D0734290

A SEASON
MOST
UNFAIR

A Season Most Unfair

J. ANDERSON COATS

Atheneum Books for Young Readers

NEW YORK LONDON TORONTO SYDNEY NEW DELHI

ATHENEUM BOOKS FOR YOUNG READERS

An imprint of Simon & Schuster Children's Publishing Division

1230 Avenue of the Americas, New York, New York 10020

Text © 2023 by J. Anderson Coats

Jacket illustration © 2023 by Matt Rockefeller

Jacket design by Debra Sfetsios-Conover © 2023 by Simon & Schuster, Inc.

ATHENEUM BOOKS FOR YOUNG READERS is a registered trademark of Simon & Schuster, Inc. Atheneum logo is a trademark of Simon & Schuster, Inc.

For information about special discounts for bulk purchases, please contact Simon & Schuster Special Sales at 1-866-506-1949 or business@simonandschuster.com.

The Simon & Schuster Speakers Bureau can bring authors to your live event. For more information or to book an event, contact the Simon & Schuster Speakers Bureau at 1-866-248-3049 or visit our website at www.simonspeakers.com.

Interior design by Irene Metaxatos

The text for this book was set in Iowan Old Style.

Manufactured in the United States of America

0523 FFG

First Edition

10 9 8 7 6 5 4 3 2 1

Library of Congress Cataloging-in-Publication Data

Names: Coats, J. Anderson (Jillian Anderson), author.

Title: A season most unfair / by J. Anderson Coats.

Description: First edition. | New York : Atheneum Books for Young Readers, 2023. | Audience: Ages 10 and up. | Summary: Scholastica, or "Tick," loves making candles in her father's shop, but when he takes on an apprentice and forbids Tick from helping, she is determined to prove she deserves a spot in his shop.

Identifiers: LCCN 2022022764 | ISBN 9781665912358 (hardcover) | ISBN 9781665912372 (ebook)

Subjects: CYAC: Fathers and daughters—Fiction. | Sex role—Fiction. | Determination—Fiction. | Candles—Fiction. | LCGFT: Historical fiction. | Novels.

Classification: LCC PZ7.1.C62 Se 2023 | DDC [Fic]—dc23

LC record available at https://lccn.loc.gov/2022022764

TO CAITLIN, CLARK,
AND MAYA

A Season Most Unfair

⇒ APRIL ⇐

1

I'M ONLY GOING out to get the fire started, but already the cats have assembled.

They are three, and they sit like points on a sundial around the huge, scarred kettle in the rear yard. I've no idea how they know, but they're right, down to the hour—today's the day Papa and I are going to start rendering tallow for our big season of candlemaking. Papa's at the butcher right now collecting the first load of fat we'll need, and the cats are very much aware there'll be scraps of meat too small to go on our table.

Big Gray is shaped like a furry beehive, and he regards me like he knows I won't be feeding him at the moment and he's judging me for it. Sunshine has yellow eyes and a stripey back, and the Fox is a deep orange with white-tipped paws. They stand on either side of Big Gray like lieutenants, or perhaps supper guests.

None of these cats belongs to me. They turn up when there's tallow bubbling, unlike, say, almost everyone else in St Neots, who keep well enough away when smoke starts rising from our yard. Papa even agreed to live on the edgemost edges of town, but even that's not enough. I'm always overhearing the very colorful and unflattering things our neighbors mutter about the smell. Or the *stink*, as some of them are unkind enough to say.

Sometimes not just about the smell of the yard. Sometimes about the smell of *me*.

Everyone likes a candle to burn when the winter closes in, though, and somehow when those candles burn, they don't smell like we do when we make them.

The kettle stays in this spot outside more or less year-round. It's so big and heavy that we don't move it unless we have to, but it's suspended on a sturdy truss so it's simple enough to kindle a fire beneath it and start water boiling.

When Papa gets here, I'll cut the fat he brings into small pieces—Big Gray and Sunshine and the Fox will be my very dearest friends for a while—and then it's just a matter of letting it render down several times so all that's left is nice, smooth tallow, which will become lovely candles.

Well. There's the matter of the smell. Honestly, though, it's not as bad as people say.

It's a bright day in spring, and a joy to sit on an upturned bucket near the kettle and watch the world go by. Mostly it's bees, with the occasional bird, until a group of children comes from town along the road that ends in fields just past my house. Lucy's little brothers and sisters, and Johanna's, too, all muddled together like usual, and they're swinging sackcloth bags and chattering like wrens.

Lucy's papa is the goldsmith, and Johanna's is a baker. We were all born the same summer, but unlike them, my house didn't fill up with so many brothers and sisters that I was all but appointed second mama. It must give them a lot to talk about. It surely gives them a lot to do.

Lucy and Johanna have their matching aprons on today, the ones with the little runner of embroidery along the waistband.

A dark-haired boy breaks away from the group and races toward me. It's Adam, one of Lucy's brothers. He's eight or so, and I figure he wants to pet the cats. I rise from my bucket and curtsy a little. "Good mor—"

"Stennnnnnnnnnnnnch!" he shrieks as he flies past the house and into the field beyond.

Sunshine hunkers, and Big Gray turns to glare.

"Stop that!" Lucy scolds, and Johanna shouts,

"Adam, you get back here and beg pardon—"

But it's too late. Adam's long gone, and the other kids are running after him, crowing *Stench!* and *What smells?* and *Get away, get away!,* all while holding their noses or pressing their bags to their faces.

Johanna trails to a stop in the road. "Tick, I must beg your pardon for that. What a little vermin he is."

"I've heard worse," I tell her, and I smile and shrug because it's true. "Going foraging?"

Spring's the hungry part of the year, the garden still greening and winter stores scraping bottom, and they're likely heading out to find chickweed, or goosegrass, or other things that grow wild and won't be missed.

Lucy's eyes go to the kettle in the yard. "Oh. Well. I . . . I suppose you could come. We'll be outside and all."

I toe the dirt, my stomach souring a little.

Big Gray winds around my legs, then starts licking my ankle. I reach down to rub his ears. No matter how many times I wash my gown and hose, or how much the cats help out, there's always tallow in the weave of everything I own.

"That's all right," I say. "Papa and I are starting our work today. I'll be all day trimming fat and minding the tallow. We have much to do to ready ourselves for the Stourbridge Fair."

It's a little mean, me adding that last part, because

neither Lucy nor Johanna gets to go to the fair. They have to watch their brothers and sisters, which is why they're always together. They've long since worked out that four hands are better than two, even when the group is bigger, and those kids mind both Johanna and Lucy without much care for who shares whose blood.

But Johanna shrugs easily and says, "Your papa's making wax charms, though, right? Perhaps you'd save me back an Agnus Dei. I could give you a braid of onions for it."

"That's my job this year," I tell her proudly, though I leave off the part where Papa can't see well enough to press the plum-sized mold against the precious beeswax, nor use the tiny brushes to paint the little lamb and his banner.

Papa says it's better if people don't know how fuzzy the world looks to him now when he tries to see things close-up.

Johanna smiles. "You've been looking forward to making charms since forever!"

"We should go." Lucy tugs Johanna's sleeve and tips her chin toward the field, where only the smallest children are still visible. "Farewell, Tick."

I wave, and I'm reaching for a new piece of firewood when Johanna turns and asks, "Who's the boy? Is he visiting? I didn't think you had any cousins."

"I don't. What boy?"

"The one I saw through the window," Johanna replies. "Your stepmother was giving him a big wedge of bread and cheese when we went past."

Lucy pulls harder on Johanna's sleeve, and together they hurry with their forage bags into the fields, where they scoop up the little kids and move in deeper to find the bigger ones.

I add some sticks to the fire. The water is getting good and hot, but I'm not thinking about that anymore. Nor the cats. Not even Papa, on his way home from the butcher.

Had it been Lucy who said it, I'd have paid it no mind. She needs to be the king in every game of king of the mountain and have the biggest blossoms in her flower crowns. But Johanna is like a daisy—everything good is drawn to her.

Still, I wait till they're both out of sight, then I head for the rear yard door, closing it tight behind me so none of the cats can get in and swipe our supper.

The boy is probably from the poorer quarter of St Neots, and Mama Elly isn't good at letting want go unanswered when it's in front of her.

The back of the house is the workshop, where Papa and I make candles. I dodge around the big rack in the middle of the room, past the deep tallow troughs, and around the pile of molds, hurrying because I can hear voices now.

Mama Elly's, and also one I don't recognize. The boy's, likely. They're happy voices, and then they laugh.

I weave through the kitchen and step into the hall, our living area at the front of the house.

Sure enough, there's a boy here.

Sure enough, he's eating a generous wedge of rye bread and fragrant cheese while making my stepmother laugh.

And I'd be all right with that, only he's sitting at the big, spacious trestle board carefully positioned under a window to catch the most light, where I do tasks like twisting wicks or painting wax charms, work that needs young eyes that aren't blurry at the edges like Papa's.

My bright table.

"Tick, my lamb!" Mama Elly swings herself up from her stool. Her leg brace scrapes the rungs. "I thought you'd gone foraging with your friends."

"Ah." I have no notion why she'd think that. She and Papa have been wed for most of my life, so she knows how he and I spend this time of year, and she should surely know Lucy and Johanna and I haven't spent more than an afternoon together since we were small. "No, of course not. I've gotten the kettle started. Papa and I will likely be rendering for the next few weeks."

Mama Elly pauses. Her face is slowly turning the kind of pink that only redheads can turn. Then she flutters a smile. "Hey, why don't you join Henry in a bit of bread? Henry, this is our Tick."

The boy is about my age, sturdy like a fencepost, with hair the color of a roebuck falling to his shoulders. He's wearing a tunic of good blue wool, orange hose that don't sag in the slightest, and fine leather boots that look like they were new-made yesterday.

When Mama Elly gestures to me, he swallows his mouthful and slides off the stool. Then he dips his chin, polite, and says, "Henry of Holgate. A pleasure to meet you."

I nod back, even though I'm not sure why we're making acquaintances if he's just come for charity, though anyone with boots like those surely doesn't need our bread. Still, I curtsy and reply, "Pleasure to meet you, too."

"Tick," he repeats, like it's a curiosity he's poking.

"From Scholastica," I explain, because I am in no humor to hear any one of the jokes that often come with my name.

Henry's brows go up. "Oh! You mean like St Benedict's sister?"

"St Scholastica was her own person, you know. Not just someone's sister."

Henry has the grace to look sheepish, which he tries to hide by dusting crumbs from his front and turning to Mama Elly. "Ah. Well. That was delicious, mistress. Thank you. Best make a good impression on the master, though, and get right to my labor. Will you show me where to begin?"

He is not staring at her leg brace. He is treating her like anyone else, like someone who could very well be the one who'd show him what's what in the rear yard.

"There'll be no mistress anything while you're beneath my roof," she scolds, but in a playful way. "It's Mama Elly to everybody, you included. Hear?"

Henry nods, smiling, but I glance between them because even though that is such a Mama Elly thing to say to anyone, there's no reason for him to be beneath our roof, and the only person he might be calling master is Papa, but Papa has no need for him because he has me.

"And if you want to know where to begin with the candlemaking, Tick's the one to ask." Mama Elly turns to me. "There's the rendering, right? Why not get him going on that?"

Because it's *my* task? Because I've minded that kettle since I was old enough to poke wood beneath its bottom and tall enough to drag a paddle through whatever was bubbling within?

But I turn to Henry and say, "Let's go out back. You can help me."

I smile again, turn on my heel, and march through the house. Henry trails after me, and I think he may be dawdling to take in the huge candle rack that fills up much of the workshop, but my hands are shaking and my belly feels as hot and runny as new-melted tallow.

The yard is just as I left it, and I make a big show of checking the height of the fire, the grid of sticks beneath the kettle, the steam rising from the water. The cats retreat when Henry follows me across the mud, but they don't go far.

"So." Henry pauses, and I can tell he's sorting through different things he can say. "Your stepmother told me you've been helping your father since you were really little."

"I have. I'm more or less his apprentice."

"Only you can't be," Henry points out, but not in a mean way. "Not really. Girls can't be apprentices in the chandler's trade."

"I know as much about candlemaking as any apprentice," I tell him.

Henry doesn't reply. Instead he reaches for my bucket, the one I sit on, and starts to turn it right side up. I whip it out of his hands, stump it firmly back in the mud the proper rump-holding way, and point at it.

"Why don't you sit there?" I say. "You can watch."

"Watch water boil?"

He's trying to make a joke, I can tell, but I'm not in any humor for jokes. This boy is not here for charity. Somehow he's gotten it into his head that my father needs an apprentice. He's even convinced Mama Elly of it, to the point that she wants me to teach him how to take my tasks away!

2

THE CREAK OF wooden wheels sends me skittering across the yard. Trudge is swaying up the road, hauling our rickety cart behind him. Papa walks at the old donkey's side, his leather apron already shiny with spilled fat. He sees me and waves, and I almost collapse in relief.

Papa will send Henry on his way, and then we can finally start our summer work. Even though the fair won't happen until the Feast of the Holy Cross in September, there's so much to do that we must start in spring, as soon as it's warm. During summer, the days will be very long and we can fit a lot of boiling and dipping and trimming in the extra daylight. Then, as the season turns, we'll pack up the cart with all those candles, give Trudge an extra share of grain, and walk the twenty miles to Stourbridge to sell the lot.

We'll sell Agnus Dei charms, too. I'll stamp each one out while sitting at my bright table, then dab them with tiny sweeps of paint. Each one will keep a traveler safe wherever the road takes them.

As Papa turns Trudge off the path, I move away from the gate so they can come into the yard. The cats are back in position around the kettle, tails curled, waiting with that eerie patience of cats.

In the cart are four bulging rucksacks already darkening with fat and suet like sweat beneath an underarm.

"The water should be just starting to boil," I tell Papa as I unwind the rope securing the wagon's tailgate. "I've got the cutting board ready, and I sharpened the knife. Carefully, like you're always telling me."

I keep glancing at Henry as I'm saying all this. Papa surely doesn't need to hear it. I know exactly what I'm supposed to do, and Papa knows I know.

"Very good, dear one." Papa holds up a greasy hand, playfully threatening to muss my hair, and I duck away, squealing with laughter. Then he turns to Henry. "You must be John's boy. I guess he got my message after all! It's been an age since I've seen you. You're almost a man! Did you have a safe journey?"

"I did, sir." Henry bows. "My father apologizes for

my lateness and sends his best regards, but he wasn't able to make the trip along with me."

"Well." Papa smiles, but it's not a whole smile. "That's a shame, but Norwich is a far piece from here. I can't afford to be so long away from my trade either."

Henry flinches the smallest bit, like he just realized he forgot to latch the byre door all the way back in Norwich. Then he says, "I'm deeply grateful that you sent for me. You won't be sorry, taking me on."

Papa laughs. "Well, I'm not getting any younger, and candlemaking is a good trade. I probably should have taken on an apprentice years ago. Work hard and do as you're told, and you'll be welcome."

My mouth falls open. My guts go leaden. Papa is not sending him away. He's not even surprised Henry is here.

He *invited* Henry. To be his apprentice.

"I'm hoping we'll manage five hundred pounds of candles for the fair. It'll be a big job of work, but a good way for you to get your feet wet, eh?" Papa claps Henry on the back, and Henry tips his chin up and smiles proudly. "Why don't you sit down, son, and we'll get you started right away."

Papa gestures toward the makeshift trestle table I've set up with the cutting board and knife.

"But . . ." I don't know where to start. There's too

much wrong. "But it's render day! I'm the one who cuts up the fat. I always get all the meat off, too. I've got everything ready, and there's no way Henry will do any of it right!"

"Not straightaway," Papa replies kindly, "but he'll learn it, same as you. No one's good at anything the first time."

I study my feet. My first few batches of candles were gruesome, reeking of meat bits still stuck in the tallow and drawing every mouse in thirty miles to take bites out of the middle, sometimes while they were still burning in their holders.

"All right. Well." I fluster with my apron ties. "I suppose I could show him how, and we could do the rendering together."

"Thank you, dear one, but I'll be showing him," Papa tells me. "Why don't you unhitch Trudge and give him some hay?"

"But Papa, you're always saying how your eyes—" I cut myself off even before Papa gives me a warning look. This John, whoever he is, clearly figured he was sending his son to be taught the trade by a chandler who could see well enough to dip candles to an even thickness or twist a wick tight enough to hold flame throughout the candle's whole life.

Henry stands by awkwardly, petting Sunshine, but

when Papa starts unloading the bags of fat and suet from the cart, he leaps up and goes to help.

"Well. What I mean is . . . ah . . ." I'm trying to finish my thought in a way that won't be a lie, but also won't make Papa look bad, when Trudge starts toward the byre all by himself. He knows the routine. Once the cart is in the yard, his labor is finished and he can rest himself.

The cart won't fit through the byre entrance, though, and Trudge has been known to drag it through anyway and shear the wheels off if you don't unhitch him fast enough.

I hurry to catch up, tethering Trudge and telling him he's a good boy when this is very much a falsehood. While I'm unbuckling the straps of his harness, I can hear Papa behind me explaining to Henry how rendering works, how long the fat must boil, how to skim off gristle, how to know it's finished.

I can't remember not knowing these things. I don't remember a summer when it wasn't Papa and me around this fire, in and out of the workshop, draping lengths of wicking over the candle racks and lowering each set into the tallow troughs again and again.

My hands are flying over the leather straps, and soon they're off the donkey's bony haunches and onto their pegs in the byre. I put both hands on Trudge's rump and all but shove him into his field, then I fling two armloads of hay into his manger before slamming the gate shut behind him.

Then I'm back in the yard just as Papa drops a bag of fat at one end of the trestle table with the cutting board, right at Henry's elbow.

Right where I usually sit.

I pull my rump bucket to the other end of the table and plant myself down. Papa frowns at me, but turns to Henry and gestures to the nearby bag. "Best way to learn is to get right to it. Reach in there and grab yourself a piece."

Henry hesitates, his nose wrinkling, and right there I see my chance. Perhaps no one's told this boy what goes into being a chandler's apprentice. Perhaps all I need to do is tell him true what his next fifty years will look like and he'll be on his way home today.

I lean forward. "Rendering tallow's going to stink up this whole yard and no one will want to be your friend ever again."

Big Gray puts a huge forepaw on my knee and swipes at my hand with the other.

"He will," Henry says with a smile.

"You'll get the best tallow when the fat is in very little pieces," Papa goes on, ignoring both me and the pushy cat. "You must cut away anything that isn't fat. Gristle. Meat."

"It's slimy, and it makes a vile sound when you hit sinew," I put in.

"Tick." Papa says it like a sigh.

I hold out my hands innocently because *someone's* got to tell Henry what he's getting himself into.

"You're not helping," Papa adds.

"I *could* be," I mutter, but I settle back on my bucket and watch as Henry fishes a chunk of fat out of the bag.

Sunshine takes the opportunity to shove her muzzle into the opening, and even though I'm tempted to let these furry wretches make off with some of the more choice morsels just to show Papa who knows what, I reach over and twist the bag closed.

Henry picks up the knife, turns the gristle chunk over a few times, then presses the tip of the blade against what's clearly fat and makes a tentative, halting cut.

"Good," Papa says, but I know he can't see a lick of what Henry is doing. The boy could be carving off his thumb and Papa wouldn't know the difference.

I watch Henry make a few more cuts. The first leaves a runner of sinew attached, and another misses a perfectly good slice of shiny fat. Big Gray twines impatiently around Henry's legs and the Fox meows in that high, demanding way of his, but the boy ignores them.

I can't take it anymore. Quick as a blink, I whip the knife and the fat chunk out of Henry's hands and start cutting it myself. I swerve the point of the knife around the grotty little bits and work out shavings of meat, which I throw up high so the cats can nab them midair.

I like cutting. It's a puzzle to work out, how to get each small bit of fat from its gaol of gristle. The pieces of fat I slice into bits the size of my pinkie fingernail and sweep into a pile for the kettle.

"See?" I say to Henry. "Like that. There are also these furry scoundrels to contend with." I gesture to the Fox and Sunshine and Big Gray, who are sniffing the mud for stray scraps. "Unless you give over the meat bits, those beasts will ruin your day trying to get them. Cats are very persistent."

"Tick!" Papa snaps, and all right, me taking the knife out of Henry's hands may have gone over the line a little.

So I hand the blade back, slow and reluctant, and tell Papa, "I was only trying to show him. It's easier to know what to do if you see it done. Like you showed me when I was small."

Papa's face softens, and perhaps goes a little embarrassed, since he can't exactly do that part himself. "Very well. You've shown him. But Henry was sent here to learn a trade properly, from a master."

For the second time today my belly goes *slosh*. I might not be a master, but I've learned the trade properly. Every bit Papa's shown me, I've done till it's right.

"Well . . . ah . . ." I rock on the bucket. "I guess it'll be all right if Henry and I work together. He can fish the gristly bits out of the kettle while I cut."

Papa shakes his head. "Doing these tasks on his own is the best way Henry will learn, and he must master these skills so he can set himself up in trade one day."

I slice a glare at Henry, but he's reaching down to stroke Big Gray's back, and I can't help but scowl, that these furry traitors have taken to this pretender already.

"Well. I see." I try for reasonable. "What am I to do, then? Shall I start twisting wicks? Cleaning the molds?"

"Henry will be taking over those tasks, too. You're to help your stepmother with the sweeping and scrubbing and such." Papa must realize that I'm about to kick like Trudge at the farrier because he adds, "I'm also hoping you'll take over the garden. It's not going to survive Eleanor's care, and you have a hand for growing things."

Papa wants me to smile at his gentle teasing of Mama Elly. She has a hard time bending because of her leg brace, which is why our garden often struggles. It's an effort for her to plant and weed, and she tends to smash seedlings by accident when she moves from row to row.

"I thought you liked to work the garden with her," I reply in a small voice.

"I do, and I will, sometimes," Papa says. "But I also must teach Henry the chandler's trade, and there are things only I can show him."

I blink hard. If there are things only Papa can teach him, it means there are things he knows that I don't.

Which means there are things he hasn't showed me.

"What about the beeswax?" I ask. "I can start on the charms like you said I could—"

"We are finished talking about this, Scholastica." Papa sounds exhausted, like we've been turning it over for ages. "Leave it, and go ask your stepmother what she wants done."

I don't hear my full name often, but when I do, I know it's time to step to whatever I've been told.

I stand up so fast that my sitting bucket tips, and I'm halfway across the yard when it occurs to me to glare once more at Henry, only when I do, he's righting my bucket with one hand and offering the Fox a piece of meat with the other.

I find Mama Elly where she almost always is—leaning over the fire. Her back is to me, and her fat red braid has come loose from its pins and lies against her shoulders. I fling myself onto the hearth bench, fold my arms, and sigh so big and gusty that she has no choice but to look up.

"I must beg your pardon, Tick. Your papa said you

knew Henry was coming." Mama Elly rests her backside against her tall stool. "I had no idea you didn't till you walked in and got an eyeful of him."

All winter, Papa went on at length about summer and the fair, like he always does, and he did say he hoped to make more candles than ever, that it would take a lot more work than usual.

I just figured that would mean staying later in the evenings in the yard or the workshop, each of us with a mug of cider, dipping the candles into the tallow row by row and talking about how many stars there were in the heavens, or exactly how many skeins of wool you could get from a ten-year-old sheep. Anything and everything.

Just the two of us.

"Don't be upset at poor Henry," Mama Elly goes on. "He's a good boy. His father and yours knew each other years ago as apprentices, and they promised that each would take the other's son into his trade one day."

"Papa doesn't have a son," I mutter, and even though my father has never once made me feel my lack of boy parts, all I can think about is how he called Henry *son* not a handful of moments ago in the yard.

"Perhaps you should count your blessings you're not a son." Mama Elly is teasing now. "John's a tanner, and if there's a trade more . . . *fragrant* than candlemaking, it's working with leather."

I run a thumb over the table's wood grain. The smell is honestly not that bad, and right now I'd give a whole lot to be up to my elbows in fat, my knife slipping through the gristle, giggling at the cats tussling over scraps, while Papa gets the big candle rack set up in the workshop, draped with dozens of twisted lengths of wick waiting to be dipped.

And if Henry grew up around a trade that's just as stinky as candlemaking—perhaps *more* so—then he's not going to be squeamish about melting a little fat in a kettle.

"It doesn't matter whether Henry's a good boy or not, or whose son he is," I grumble. "He has no idea what he's doing, and he's only going to slow Papa down. Without my help, Papa won't be able to make enough candles to turn a tidy penny at the fair, which means we won't have as much coin as usual, which means we'll go hungry all winter. I don't want to starve just because some bumblefingers doesn't know fat from sinew!"

Mama Elly is trying not to smile. "Your papa's a good teacher. I'm sure Henry will pick things up quickly, and there'll be plenty of candles to sell at the fair."

I fold my arms on the trestle board and lower my cheek onto them. The world goes dark.

Henry's here for good. Papa didn't even have the courtesy to tell me he was coming. There's five hundred pounds of candles that need making before the Stourbridge Fair, and beeswax charms to press and paint, and instead of telling me to roll up my sleeves and help, my father relegated me inside to sweep and tidy like girls who've never been taught to trim wicks and measure alum.

"Papa says to ask what you need done." I say it glumly into the table.

There's a scraping of wood on packed earth, then a soft, warm weight on my back. Mama Elly rubs my shoulders in a calming, comforting way till I look up at her.

"I could use some freshly foraged greens for the pottage," she says in a knowing, sly way, and she tips her chin at the front door that leads to the road outside, where not long ago Lucy and Johanna passed by.

I put my head back down. Needing greens is not a falsehood, not exactly, and I know very well that Mama Elly is trying to rub salve into this sting to take away some of the poison.

"A girl should have friends," she adds in a voice that's so quiet and sad that I don't think it's meant for me. Mama Elly doesn't talk about her childhood much, but given how she was born with one leg shorter than the other, it's not hard to guess how most kids treated her.

And here I am, facedown on her newly wiped trestle table, dragging my feet when she's nudging me toward an afternoon in the glorious April sun with girls I used to spend every waking moment with when we were in diapers.

Two girls who have matching aprons now, while mine is spattered with tallow and covered in cat hair.

Still, I push the bench back, mumble goodbye to Mama Elly, and drag into the workshop to collect a bag.

By chance I catch sight of Henry in the yard bent over the cutting board, Papa kneeling close and no doubt squinting so he can offer advice that makes sense. Already the smell of rendering fat is everywhere, and even though I'm not a stone's throw from them, I feel so very far away.

I am close enough, however, to notice how the bag of fat at Henry's side is still bulging, and the other three are knotted shut. Henry is cutting, careful and diligent, but that means he's going slower than slow. I'd be halfway through the bag by now, and Papa could be setting up the candle rack without needing to hover and watch.

But no.

It's got to be Henry, and already the day is getting ahead of us.

Only that's when I take heart. Papa's always saying that some lessons you have to teach yourself. This is what he tells me when I do things like eat too many gooseberries and get a bellyache and then spend half a day in the yard privy.

By the end of the day, Papa will see that Henry isn't cut out to be a chandler's apprentice. Henry may be a nice boy, but nice doesn't mean he can work as fast as I can, or as well.

There's a reason Papa and I spend all spring and summer making candles well into the evenings, using every last bit of the day—Stourbridge Fair is where we make most of a year's living. People come from every corner of the realm, and also from other realms beyond the Narrow Seas, and they come ready to spend.

Our candles might be simple, but they're within the means of most people, and they're of good quality. We dip them steady and even, giving plenty of time for the layers to dry thoroughly, so they burn bright and slow. You can buy one, or you can buy a pound, and each will be the same as the last.

Papa might trade twenty pounds of candles for a healthy pig, and that'll be our meat till Christmas. Or he might take a fat gold coin the size of my palm with some foreign king's head on one side, which he'll trade to Lucy's papa for sacks of barley. We'll come home with chickens in wicker cages and bags bulging with turnips and bricks of salt and Papa's purse jangling.

There's no better feeling than seeing the top of the house edge into view on a bright September evening after all that walking. Smoke rising from the roof vent, which means Mama Elly has something hot on for supper.

Your feet are sore and you're sweaty and rumpled and tired, but the cart that you're walking beside has goods enough to keep the people in your family and all the animals healthy and sound through winter, well past the hungry times of spring.

That's because of you and your endless work, and that makes every little hardship worth it. The tallow burns on your arms. The smell in your hair. The dim of the workshop, when summer was in full, glorious bloom just beyond the door. Worth it, every last bit, knowing you had a hand in keeping your family in bread.

I look down at the bag I'm holding. Then out the door once again, at Henry still cutting that same piece of fat.

By sundown, Papa will have to accept the truth. Without me, Stourbridge Fair will be a disaster.

But he will ask Mama Elly if I did as she bade me, and if I don't, it'll be that much harder to shine myself up as a good girl.

Which means I'd best get foraging.

3

BETWEEN THEM, Lucy and Johanna have ten brothers and sisters, so finding them would be simple. All I'd have to do is follow the trail of trampled grass, broken branches, muddy footprints, and wilting flowers that were picked and then dropped.

Still, it takes me several long moments to decide if I want to.

There was a time when the three of us went everywhere together. We threw sticks for dogs and splashed in the mud and played hide-and-seek all over St Neots. When Lucy turned up one day with her little sister, it was the more the merrier. Same with Johanna's small brother a few months later.

But young kids don't always play right, and they need

naps and kisses on their skinned knees and sometimes they just throw tantrums and there's no consoling them, so the game has to stop while you sort them out.

After a while I started staying home more, wandering the rear yard and dragging a stick behind me, singing ballads I only half knew and making up words when I couldn't remember them.

One day I meandered over to Papa, up to his elbows in tallow, and asked what he was doing. He set me to work minding the kettle, and even though watching fat bubble might sound as dull as dishwater, I liked being in charge of something. I liked that Papa trusted me enough to give me a task.

The next time Johanna came to the door and asked if I could come out to play, I proudly told her I couldn't. There was too much work to do, and my papa couldn't do without me, especially not for a morning's hide-and-seek.

She and Lucy both kept coming by for a while, but I hardly noticed when they stopped. My candles were getting better with every batch. Soon they'd be good enough to sell.

That September was my first trip to the Stourbridge Fair. As Papa and I rolled out of St Neots, I waved joyfully from my place at Trudge's bridle, but only Johanna waved back. Lucy was holding a baby on one arm and a little one's sleeve with her other hand.

Neither of them was smiling.

Then it felt like every time I saw one of my friends, I'd see the other. Lucy and Johanna were their own small army, and it seemed like every other month, there was another little kid on someone's hip or clinging to her skirts. I'd wave, they'd wave, and off we'd go in different directions.

Now it's been so long that it's hard to know what to say when I do see them. Even on a bright day in April when the world is turning green again, the kind of day we all used to bask in like kittens in a patch of sun.

I'm kneeling to pull some chickweed when I see a small foot.

My heart judders, and I'm almost too frightened to go over to the hedge it's sticking out of. But then the foot shifts slow and drifty, and I can breathe again. There's a little boy asleep in the shade, wrapped in a cloak. He's perhaps two, and I recognize him as Johanna's smallest brother. I think he's called Waleran.

It's perfectly quiet but for the wind gently shushing and the bees and birds and small, scurrying creatures waking up. No kids chattering or squealing or yelling *stench*. No Lucy telling them to behave. No Johanna distracting them with a game.

I stand there, just looking at him. He seems content

enough, but he's so small, and he's all by himself.

I have no memory of my mother, but I was about this size when she died. Only months larger when Papa remarried. Mama Elly is always saying how taken she was by me, how she never thought she'd get to be anyone's mama and yet here I was.

A baby who needed a mama. Who needed *her*.

Soon Waleran will wake up and find himself alone, and I don't like that thought. I also don't want to sit here waiting for him to stir, so there's nothing to do but bring him to Lucy and Johanna.

I drape the forage bag over my shoulder, kneel, and slide one arm beneath his shoulders and the other under his rump. He's warm, like a little loaf of bread, and surprisingly squishy. Like holding Big Gray when he'll allow it.

Surely Waleran will keep sleeping while I follow the trail of destruction to find his brothers and sisters. I'll lay him against my shoulder where he'll doze prettily, and when Johanna sees, she'll marvel at how good I am with babies even though it's just me at home.

I haven't quite straightened when Waleran opens big dark eyes. Slow at first, slow and sleepy, but then he realizes I'm not Johanna. I'm not even Lucy.

And he starts to scream.

For a long moment I'm stunned still, like I've been

caught midfelony and the bailiff will pop out of the brush and blister my ears for picking up someone else's baby brother and making him cry.

Then I jerk into motion, hurrying along the muddy path head down like a caught-out cutpurse. I'm all but running, and the jouncing ride isn't making Waleran any happier. He's pushing away from me as much as he can, his little arms stiff as firewood, and he arches his back like a cat does when you're foolish enough to try to pick it up unawares. He's loud like a cat, too, bawling like I'm murdering him with every step.

Sure enough, they're by the stream, and Waleran's noise brings several little kids rushing toward me, looking worried. Lucy and Johanna are close behind, but once they see it's me, they seem more puzzled than anything.

I hold out the screeching, flailing Waleran, and Johanna takes him on her hip and coos to him and pets his thatchy forelock, and slowly he quiets into snuffles, clinging to her shoulder with both hands clenched into her gown.

"You woke him up, didn't you?" Lucy asks. "Why'd you do that?"

"I must beg your pardon," I mumble. "I saw him sleeping there all by himself, and I was worried that no one knew where he was."

Lucy sighs. "We do this all the time. The small ones

know they can just lie down when they're sleepy, and when they wake, they call out and someone goes to find them. What, do you think we left him alone on purpose?"

My face feels hot. I figured they'd all tumbled off to the next patch of goosegrass and no one noticed he wasn't among them, but Lucy is sure to take offense if I say as much.

"Well, no harm done. Waleran's just fine, isn't he?" Johanna bounces the baby on her hip, then turns to me. "It's nice to see you, but I thought you said you'd be busy all day with the candlemaking."

I hesitate just long enough for Lucy to pounce on it.

"It's that boy, isn't it?" She swings her half-full forage bag and smiles like she just won a footrace. "He's your father's new apprentice, and you've been shown the door."

It's one thing to feel it bumping around inside you like a fly swallowed by mischance. Another thing entirely for someone to say it out loud. Especially someone like Lucy, who enjoys knowing things of this sort the way some people like having a coin in their purse.

"I don't mean anything by it," she adds. "It was going to happen sooner or later. You knew that, right?"

"No!" I cinch my arms over my front, staunch, like Trudge digging in his heels. "I just . . . Mama Elly's leg is troubling her, and I thought to cheer her up with something fresh to eat. Papa said I could if I was quick."

This is an absolute falsehood without even the shine of truth. Lucy folds her arms and peers at me like I'm the hairiest bug, but Johanna says, "Hey, I know! It's almost time for our midday meal. Tick can eat with us. Your parents wouldn't mind, would they, Tick? It's been *forever* since we've sat at table together."

"You just want an Agnus Dei." Lucy rolls her eyes and gently shoves Johanna. "Can't imagine why. You never go anywhere."

I flinch—that feels mean, even for someone with a tongue as sharp as Lucy's—but Johanna only puts out her own tongue and replies, "It also protects against bad influences. Which sounds a bit like *someone* I know."

Lucy cackles and starts herding children. Johanna does the same, and a hollow opens up within me, watching them work together. How easily they share jokes and tease, how their work no longer seems like work when they do so.

It's how Papa and I are when we're in the workshop.

Only today I'm not in the workshop. Henry is.

Soon enough the lot of us are heading back toward St Neots. Lucy is a generous arm's length from me, while Johanna is trying to balance her distance. The bigger kids are well ahead, holding their noses and giggling.

We'll have to pass our house to get into town, and we're sure to see Henry. He'll still be working on that first bag of fat when his beard comes in.

He'll spot us walking by. He'll lift a hand in that maddeningly cheerful way and Lucy will turn to me and say—

I clear my throat. "The boy's name is Henry. His papa and mine are friends, and he's here to see whether the chandler's trade is for him. I doubt he'll be here long, though. Between us, he's pretty bad at it."

"Will he be staying long enough to go to the fair?" Johanna asks.

That possibility hadn't occurred to me, and now it's all I can think of. Instead of just me and Papa sharing jokes and travel bread, it would be the three of us. Papa telling me to give Henry a turn holding Trudge's bridle.

Papa clapping Henry on the back and calling him *son*.

"I—I don't think so," I finally manage. "I doubt Henry will stay longer than a fortnight."

"You're always saying how much help your papa needs at the fair," Johanna goes on. "How important it is for you to go with him. I'd think that having another—"

"Can we not talk about the fair?" Lucy grumbles.

Or Henry, I want to add, but I don't. I know Lucy well enough to understand it'd be all we'd talk about for the rest of the day.

Johanna's the one who brought up the fair, though. She really wants to go. Just once, she's always saying. Which is why she's often nudging me to tell about it, every note of music and whiff of marzipan and flip of a trained mink, so she can close her eyes and feel like she's there beside me.

The fair is the best part of the whole year. Better than Michaelmas, when everyone can eat as much meat as they want. Better than Whitsuntide, when there are days and days of bonfires and music and merrymaking and kids get to stay up late.

The Stourbridge Fair is every holy day and festival crammed onto a common all at once, then doubled and doubled again. There's a thousand-thousand things to see and smell and taste and buy, so much you can't even see all of it in the three days it runs.

One year a tumbling troupe chose me out of the crowd, and I got to crouch like a curled-up bug on a spangly yellow mat while they did leaps and twirls and tuck-and-rolls over my bent back. The crowd cheered so loud I thought their throats would fall to shreds.

When the show ended, the leader of the troupe, a broad man with brown skin and deep dimples and a gold ring in his ear, gave me a new silver penny for what he called my trouble, but between the cheering and the silky feel of the mat beneath my hands and the whish of people leaping over me and being square in the middle of it all—I admit I know something of trouble, and those few moments were definitely no trouble at all.

Sure enough, Henry waves at us from the yard as we pass the house, and I'm feeling generous enough to wave back along with Lucy and Johanna. Mercifully, they don't say anything about him and how he's sitting on my bucket holding my knife and feeding my cats.

The younger kids range around us like a cloud, swinging their forage bags. There's not enough fat in the kettle for the yard to smell strong yet, and the little ones forget to yell *stench* because the older ones are ahead by a stone's throw.

Lucy and Johanna are talking about what to make with the greens they've gathered and can they give me a share, and they're both walking close-ish to me now and it's nice, I have to admit, not worrying about whether my dress needs yet another washing.

Johanna lives in a sturdy house near the high street. I haven't been here in years, but it's just as I remember. Pretty whitewashed timbers and bright, golden thatch, the front door stained a deep, vivid orange.

As we're nearing the house, Johanna's papa steps out the orange door and closes it behind him. The kids cheer and rush him in a mob, and he pretends to fend them off even as he grabs this one, then that one, swinging them playfully as they squeal with joy.

I can't help but smile because it's the sort of thing he did when Lucy and Johanna and I were small, and I can still remember being dangled wrist-and-ankle over a horse trough while I screamed in equal measures terror and delight, even though I knew he wouldn't dream of dropping me.

Johanna rushes to her papa, too, arms thrown wide in a hug shape and heading for his middle, but he gets this look on his face like he swallowed something too big for his gullet, and he stops her at arm's length with an awkward pat to the shoulders that he seems to intend as a hug.

"Very good, my daughter." He glances around as he says it, like someone is listening even though the street is empty but for all the kids and an old woman taking some sun. "Go help your mother now."

Then he pats Johanna's head like she's a spaniel and strides away toward the priory, or perhaps the market square, or perhaps just *away*.

Johanna's arms drop to her sides. She watches his back grow smaller, then she turns to Lucy, who's shooing kids through the orange door, and says, "See? It's like this all the time now."

"Saints," Lucy murmurs, and she shifts to give Johanna the hug her father dodged. "Is he wroth about something? Can you beg his pardon?"

"I don't think so." Johanna toes the dirt. "I asked Mama if she could talk to him for me, but she said Papa just . . . he says I'm growing up. Whatever that means."

"Growing up means your papa doesn't want to hug you anymore?" I ask, and they both look at me like they forgot I was here.

"Let's go eat!" Johanna says, too brightly. "There's pottage and a whole pile of day-old bread ends. Unless the kids got to them already."

Johanna's mama greets me kindly and asks why she hasn't seen me around for so long. She is with child again, which makes me think of the growing-up talk Mama Elly stumbled through this winter, which gave me way more detail than I wanted on the subject and convinced me well enough never to look twice at any boy.

I take the spoon Johanna's mama offers me and join the others around the pottage pot. I do manage to secure a bread end at great risk to my hand, given how fast the little ones are grabbing them despite Lucy's scoldings to share and be generous to their guest.

Johanna isn't eating with the rest of us, though. She and her mama are whispering in the corner.

Her father doesn't love her any less. It's just that there were people watching, and they could get the wrong idea. Better to be more circumspect. Perhaps only curtsy next time.

Johanna is rounder in her womanly places than either Lucy or me. Lucy is skinny like a half-dipped candle, while I'm as sturdy and blocky as a cat in winter fettle.

I put down my spoon as it dawns on me, what happened earlier.

Mama Elly's growing-up talk was mainly aimed at telling me that boys would start to notice me once I became young-womanly. They would want to hug me and other things besides, but I didn't have to let them put their hands on me if I didn't want them to.

My papa doesn't count as a boy when it comes to hugs. I will always want him to hold me tight. I will never get too old for that.

Only what if he doesn't feel the same way? What if he's like Johanna's papa and won't want to hug me once I'm growing in all my growing-up places?

I turn my bread end over and over. It was hard won, but I give it to Waleran, who wisely crams it into his mouth even as two bigger hands grab for it.

My stomach is growing more hurty by the moment. Right now, Henry is standing in my stead in the workshop. He's learning the things that Papa didn't think to teach me.

Or didn't want to.

Without those things, though—without candlemaking—Papa and I won't have much to talk about.

The longer it's Henry next to him instead of me, the more likely it'll be that Papa will forget how interesting and helpful I am, and how much he needs me to make candles and wax charms and keep us all in bread.

Soon enough, the pottage is gone and Johanna is tucking Waleran into the cradle beneath the eave for a nap, his chubby legs hanging over the side. He's soon to be dismissed from it, poor little soul.

As Johanna coos a lullaby to him, Lucy turns to me. "Did you really mean it? About Mama Elly and gathering greens? Because it's just . . . Jo thought it would be fun to take the kids out to the mill and watch the paddle wheel while we forage. You could come along."

She says it like she kind of wishes I'd agree. Like the years will melt away and it'll be the three of us again, linking arms and telling jokes and sharing ribbons.

And I hesitate. I really do.

But all I can think about is Henry in my rear yard, bobbling my knife, feeding those shameless furry felons and winning their black hearts, mangling perfectly good chunks of fat and setting our work back by days and sennights.

Lucy must see it in my face because her frown tightens up, where only moments ago she was soft with hope. She turns on her heel and she is off, weaving through kids and out the front door.

I wish I could make Lucy understand, and Johanna, too, that it's not that I don't *want* to gather greens with them.

It's that Lucy called her *Jo,* and now I feel like a hidebound old aunt who insists on using someone's whole long, clunky name when there's a nickname that everybody knows.

It's that Mama Elly won't like the idea of Henry leaving. She always wanted a houseful of children, so she fusses over anyone and everyone, down to kittens and rabbits and small, scootching caterpillars.

It's being sent to gather greens when there's work to be done, and all at once there's someone better suited than me to do my work just because he's someone Papa can call *son*.

4

USUALLY DURING candlemaking season Papa and I eat our supper in the rear yard while hovering over our work. Mama Elly isn't fond of this—she prefers us to eat at the table like a family—but she puts up with it because it's important to get use out of every last bit of daylight.

So I'm not surprised at all when Mama Elly calls me over and puts two steaming bowls of pottage into my hands.

Right away I brighten. Clearly, Papa has seen the light and asked for me to come help because he realizes he's already behind.

But then I see the trestle board behind her laid with two places, and a long, slow pour of boiling water fills my belly.

"Run those out to your father and Henry," Mama Elly says, as if she's forgotten entirely that I'm the one who ought to be there helping.

When I step into the rear yard, Papa and Henry are standing over the kettle that's gently bubbling with rendered tallow.

". . . decent enough for a first try," Papa is saying, and I sigh because if it had been *me* doing the cutting, that tallow would be better than decent. "So what I'll have you do is skim those last bits of gristle, then load the tallow into these buckets. We'll bring them inside and cover them, then tomorrow we'll do a few more renderings and I'll show you how to pass the tallow through cheesecloth."

Henry nods and reaches for the metal skimmer and one of the leather buckets.

I stand there holding supper like some kind of servant girl.

Papa sees me and smiles. "I think we'll eat inside with you and Eleanor tonight. Being as it's Henry's first day with us and all."

I'm not sure what I like least—that Papa is suggesting that Henry will have a second day, or that I will never get to eat outside again, or that Henry is somehow part of our family now and gets a place at our table.

"That's a lovely idea," Mama Elly says when I relate

this to her, and she points me toward our crockery shelf to fetch two more mugs. I groan again, but quieter this time, because if there's one thing Mama Elly can't stand, it's unkindness.

Soon enough we're all sitting around the table, only it's strange now. It used to be that Mama Elly sat at one end and Papa sat at the other, and there I was in the middle, cozy like a pea in a pod, and across from me I could see my bright table tucked under the window.

Only now I can't see my bright table, because Henry is sitting across from me. He's scrubbed especially well, looking a little uncomfortable on the bench.

Since I know the bench is only a normal amount of uncomfortable, he must be feeling strange about sitting with us. No matter how welcoming Mama Elly might be, Henry is still far from home and his mama and papa, and he likely won't be seeing them for some time. He must miss those things already, even with something good in hand. I know I would.

"A fine day's work, wouldn't you say?" Papa asks Henry, and he sounds so well and truly genuine that I nearly drop my spoon.

"Fine?" I repeat. "Three bags of fat still to cut and no candles made, and that's *fine*?"

"You can't always measure good by what's made and sitting in front of you," Papa replies. "Today's good was in Henry's learning; how well he listened and how much better he was by day's end."

Henry sits up a little straighter. His cheeks are pink, and he's smiling in this shy, proud way. Mama Elly leans over to pat his elbow and coo at him.

Never mind that Papa once said the same of me, of my learning. Never mind that no one is good at anything right away.

This is completely different.

I sink back and let my shoulders fold forward like a bag of fat. A *full* one, sitting untouched.

Papa is happy with Henry's work. Mama Elly is happy to have one more soul to pet and fuss over.

Henry is clearly not going anywhere, no matter how terrible he is at chandling.

"After supper, we'll clear a space in the workshop," Papa tells Henry. "We'll get you a nice pallet and—"

"You will do no such thing!" Mama Elly cuts in. "There is no way any child is sleeping in that drafty, dusty place, not while I have a say."

"Eleanor, come now. He's an apprentice, and it's—"

"I said no!" Mama Elly jabs a spoon at Papa. "He's the son of your oldest friend, and he will be sleeping in this house just like the rest of us."

Henry shifts uncomfortably. "I don't mind, mistress. Really."

"Well, where do you suggest he sleep?" Papa turns to gesture around our hall that's already crowded with trunks and tables and bags of candle ends needing to be melted and reused.

"There's plenty of space in the loft," Mama Elly replies. "There's no reason Tick can't share."

Because the loft is *mine*? Because it's not Mama Elly's to give away and no one even *asked* me?

Papa's mouth opens. Then closes. Pink is creeping into his cheeks through his beard. "That doesn't seem . . . suitable."

"They are *children*, Osbert! Hardly more than babies. And you can't really think your good friend's son is capable of anything even somewhat inappropriate." Her eyes narrow. "Can you?"

Papa mumbles something. Henry is frozen on the bench with his spoon in his supper, and for the first time since I laid eyes on him, I feel like we are in complete agreement on something.

Neither of us wants to share my loft.

Mama Elly isn't done with Papa yet. "Besides, I know for certain you wouldn't want Tick to be relegated to some forgotten place if she were someone's apprentice. You'd want her to feel fully a part of the family, just like a daughter."

"But she'd never . . ." Papa runs a hand through his

hair, and I feel that familiar slosh in my guts.

Only now I'm not just thinking of how I'm not a real apprentice. I'm also thinking about what happened today at Johanna's house, how your papa starts looking at you differently when you become young-womanly.

"Then it's settled," Mama Elly says firmly. "Henry is part of our family now. Tick, you don't mind sharing the loft, do you?"

I *don't* want to share, and not just because Henry is all but a stranger. Because now there's no other answer than *of course I don't mind*, which means Mama Elly is forcing my hand—and my goodwill.

It's rare that I'm upset with Mama Elly, but right now I can barely look at her.

After supper Mama Elly hobbles around the hall, piling blankets and bedclothes into Henry's outstretched arms. Papa sits himself by the hearth and cuts measures of cord for unraveling and twisting into wicks. It's something that doesn't need good eyes, because you measure along the length of your arm, snip-snip.

I'm left to rinse the bowls and spoons and put them away on their shelf, which I do every night, but on this one I feel like a servant.

When I'm done, I take myself outside, find my rump bucket—turned wrong way around *again!*—and sit alone in the cooling spring air.

The only thing that still gives me any hope is how terrible Henry is at the very simplest things that go into candlemaking. He may decide of his own accord to go back home and take up the trade of tanning leather, since Papa has no son to send to Henry's father.

Soon enough the chill becomes outright cold and chases me back into the house, where everyone is gathered around the hearth. I don't look at any of them, only make a procession of me, myself, and I across the room and up the ladder to my loft, where I crawl into bed and shiver until the bedclothes warm up.

Well. Not *my* loft. Like so many things around here, what's mine is no longer mine.

Before long, Henry appears at the top of the ladder with a mighty roll of woolens under one arm. He freezes, then moves toward the end of the loft opposite mine, near the smaller window.

"This isn't my idea," Henry says. "I honestly don't mind sleeping in the workshop."

"You might, come winter," I reply, and even as it's leaving my mouth, I realize what I'm saying. What I'm agreeing is going to happen whether I like it or not.

That Henry is Papa's real, proper apprentice, and he's here to stay.

That Lucy was right, and I've been shown the door.

Henry makes himself a pallet at the end of the loft

farthest from me. Years ago, Papa hung a curtain around my bed to keep the heat in during the winter. I draw it now and wish it was made of stone.

In Mama Elly's growing-up talk, she warned me to be careful if I decided to be alone with a boy. That most boys were nice and wouldn't dream of bringing me to harm, but it was all too easy to let feelings tumble out of control.

She clearly doesn't think Henry counts as a boy. She said we were children, and if I'm honest, I'm more than a little glad to hear her say it. Being young-womanly seems to come with a lot of hassles and headaches that I want no part of.

You lose a lot of things, too, seems like. Your freedom. Your peace of mind.

Your papa.

Across the room, Henry clears his throat. "For what it's worth, I'm sorry this is happening to you. I never meant for my gain to become your loss."

I shuffle my curtain aside. The loft is dim, but I can make out the shape of him, sitting cross-legged on a pitiful pile of blankets while I perch my rump on braided hemp pulled taut in a wooden frame.

"You can be mad at me if it'll help." Henry smiles halfway. "Then I won't miss my sister quite as much."

I peer at him. It's not who I expected him to miss.

Most boys our age roam St Neots in packs, like dogs, and find girls interesting only for how loud they scream when rotting fruit is thrown at them.

"We were born not quite a year apart," Henry adds, "so it's almost like we're twins. She's called Margaret."

There's a pause, and I know he's waiting for me to ask about her. About anything, really. Where he comes from. What his parents are like. Even what he thinks about his first day of candlemaking, or of us here, of Papa and Mama Elly and those furry fair-weather friends who twine around your legs in the rear yard.

None of this is his fault, but I can't bring myself to be like Mama Elly and bubble over with warmth and hugs and the coziest of welcomes.

And it might not be his fault, but it doesn't change how tomorrow he'll be sitting at my trestle, holding my knife.

Being Papa's son.

So I don't ask about Margaret. I don't ask anything. I pull my curtain closed with a single, firm *shuff*.

It's quiet for so long that I'm sure Henry has gone to sleep, when I hear a tiny sound in the darkness. It's like a kitten, high and sad, and I realize that it's Henry.

He's crying.

I lie very still. He must think I'm asleep, because most boys I know don't like other people to know they cry.

Henry turned up here on his own. He said himself that his father couldn't make the journey. His parents just sent him off, and now he's here.

All alone, but for us.

Henry only cries for a short while, but every little snuffle and sob feels like a poke to a healing bruise.

I suppose perhaps maybe possibly it wouldn't hurt for me to ask about his sister and his home.

It wouldn't hurt for me to show him a little more kindness.

⇒MAY⇐

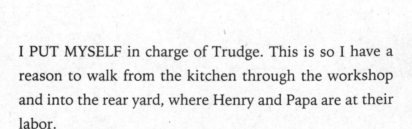

5

I PUT MYSELF in charge of Trudge. This is so I have a reason to walk from the kitchen through the workshop and into the rear yard, where Henry and Papa are at their labor.

It is precisely eight and twenty steps from the back door to the byre, and I can get within two arm's lengths of the kettle before Papa shoos me along.

Trudge's primary virtue is how little fussing he needs. Give him a manger full of hay in the morning and a byre that lets him get out of the weather when he wants, and he's happy to spend his time cropping grass in his field and passing wind.

I learn the hard way that Trudge does not appreciate someone being in charge of him. Anyone walking toward him is usually coming to put the harness on his back, and he is only reluctantly bribed to be still with a carrot or wedge of turnip.

Trudge does not like being curried. He bites the brush in half, then spends the rest of the day spitting out bristles. I spend the rest of the day making a new brush so I don't get barked at for letting him ruin the old one.

He will tolerate wearing a flower crown, but he definitely objects to having his tail braided, and he has *no intention* of learning tricks.

Still, I keep at it. Every time I walk toward him is another chance for Papa to ask me to stop and help.

I won't hold a grudge, either. I'll smile and sit down next to Henry while the smell of tallow works its way through my hair.

I will do every task cheerfully, down to the worst ones. Even mixing varnish with that awful bone glue that sticks to my fingers for ages, no matter how much I scrub them with sand.

Every time is another chance for Papa to remember how interesting my questions are, how they make him put a hand to his bristly chin and really consider his answer.

Why, no, Tick, I have no idea why we must talk to the bees, only that we must. I do wonder whether the moon is solid like a rock, or crumbly like a plowed field.

What do you think?

In the rear yard Henry works his way slowly through the bag of fat. The cats are not pleased. They've stopped their *I love you* shin-rubbing and now sit in the shade, raising dust with ever-lashing tails and judging him silently.

Sunshine and the Fox and Big Gray are patient. They can wait an age by a mouse hole, or for a bird to forget they're hiding in a dapple of shade and flutter to the ground.

I can take a lesson from them. All I must do is stand by while the pile of candles fails to grow like Papa hoped. Soon enough, he'll realize he was wrong about needing my help. He'll see the wisdom in my idea, that the three of us make candles together.

On Sunday we go to Mass. It's hard for Mama Elly to walk long distances, so Papa hitches Trudge to the cart. He lifts an eyebrow when he sees Trudge's half-braided tail, and I think he might smile a little.

I wait for him to ask the obvious question—*what is this about?*—because then I can explain how well I've been looking after Trudge. But instead Papa asks Henry to lead the donkey to the front of the house so it's easier for Mama Elly to climb into the cart, and reminds him to put her tall stool in as well so she can lean against it during the service.

I like the Mass. I like how it brings most everyone in

St Neots together, and I like hearing Father Leo's rich, beautiful voice singing the prayers. I don't even mind standing the whole time. I especially like how once it's over, the kids rush in a great swarm to the churchyard to play hoodman blind and fox-and-geese while the grown-ups mill around the portal steps to chatter and gossip and hear the news.

As we arrive at St Mary's, Mama Elly insists that Henry should stand next to her during Mass and I stand next to him, with Papa on my other side.

"So everyone knows Henry is part of the family," she explains, and his ears turn pink, but he smiles, too.

It stings, but I remember my promise to be kinder to him, so I try not to roll my eyes too hard while I wrestle Mama Elly's tall stool out of the wagon.

We're late, as usual, and Father Leo is already singing the Gloria when we rattle into the church and take up our customary spot in the back of the nave. Mama Elly tells people it's so she doesn't disturb the Mass by scrape-thudding her brace over the flagstones, but I'm not fool enough that I don't notice people leaning or shuffling or outright stepping away from Papa and me.

Today there are only a few wrinkled noses and a muffled, long-suffering sigh. Probably because it's still May and candlemaking season has only just begun. At least no one is yelling *stench*.

They're thinking it, though.

It's cool in the church despite the crammed-in people, and my eye keeps wandering to the tall, narrow windows that let in winks of the bright blue day outside. Before long my mind has wandered where it always goes this time of year—the Stourbridge Fair.

It's a modest fair, not nearly the massive sprawling one at St Ives that happens at Eastertide, but Papa says even if that one is closer, it's better to be a big fish in a small pond. Besides, the Stourbridge Fair is just outside Cambridge, and both scholars and masters there go through a lot of candles, so there are always plenty of eager buyers.

I've been to the Stourbridge Fair enough years that I've developed a particular way to enjoy it. The fair lasts for three days, and Papa and I always get there a day early, to pay the lepers and set up our booth. The fair is how the monks who keep the leper hospital make money to run the place, by charging the likes of us to set up a booth on its outskirts.

But once the booth is set up, the horsehide tent overhead and the counter laid out on low trusses, the curtain blocking our sleeping area and our pallets settled, I'm free, and I make the most of it.

The first thing to look at is always the animals. There are rabbits to hold, chickens to giggle at, and horses to admire. If you are polite and cheerful and moderately persistent, some of the horsemongers will heft you up and let you sit on the back of a placid mare or gelding, to show off its temperament. One year I was allowed to ride a pony in a big circle so the buyer could see her gait.

After you've had your fill of animals, you walk down a big thoroughfare formed by booths set up along either side. It's called Garlic Row, and you could roll four wagons along it, two going up and two going down, but there are too many people to make room for wagons.

Papa always gives me a few farthings to spend, so there's the weighty decision of whether to buy a hair ribbon or a fritter or a delightfully annoying reed whistle that will scatter the cats in the most amusing way, until it dissolves from all the spit.

The wardens of the fair decided long ago which traders can set up where, and every year they return to the same place. Each group has its own row where like goods are gathered with like, so new traders know exactly where to set stakes.

You'll find iron and pottery up near the river, and every kind of cloth you can think of at the other end of Garlic Row, near the road to the leper hospital. You'll find furs and books and toys and leather and almost everything in between, all laid out in rows that are begging to be explored.

There are also people who ply their trades right in front of you—farriers trimming hooves, smiths repairing buckles, wheelwrights replacing spokes, barbers pulling teeth—and they have little stalls away from the tents and rows, to keep down the risk of fire.

Stourbridge Fair may not be grand, but it's growing, and last year there were nearly twice as many new traders— potters, weavers, furriers, fruiterers, cordwainers, smiths, costermongers. The wardens promised to set up twice as many privies since the long lines made everyone complain, buyers and sellers alike.

Once you've admired all the things for sale, you're drawn to the music and dancing and mummery going on in the fields just beyond the stalls. You can watch tumbling troupes and trained marmosets jumping through hoops, and there's always friars there, trying to preach over one another in competingly louder voices until someone heckles them into moving to opposite corners of the field. Once there was a wrestling match to determine which friar would get to stay and who had to pack up his paternoster and leave town.

After that first day it's all business, and Papa and I sell our candles till they're gone. Sometimes it's for coins, sometimes for trade. Papa always says I'm good at the counter, that customers see a face like mine and trust me to be honest.

I like making candles, but I *really* like selling them. The fair is one of the only times I'm allowed to raise my voice and bellow as loud as I want, to call everyone close to see our candles.

I like standing behind the counter and smiling at housewives and tenant farmers, townspeople and merchants, young and old, pale and brown. I know everyone in St Neots, and I like how at Stourbridge, I get to meet people I've never seen or heard. I like how their voices are all different, their eyes and hair and skin and manners none the same. I even like haggling, and I'm not offended when someone tries to get the better of me. It's like a game, and there are only ever a few who are truly nasty about it.

For those folks, you just say you'll call the levelookers. No one wants to run afoul of the big men with cudgels that the leper hospital hires to keep order in the market and make sure no one cheats, steals, forestalls, undercuts, regrates, or otherwise tries to get something for other than what it's worth.

I might be stuck in the garden all summer, but at least come fair time, I'll be right next to Papa just like always. In our tent, behind our counter. Henry might be there, too, but not even he can ruin Stourbridge Fair.

I'm all but wriggling as Father Leo chants the post-communion, and as he dismisses us with the ite, missa est, I fling myself out the door and down the portal steps into the sunshine.

I'm not the only one. Kids tumble past me, flooding the churchyard, screeching and shouting like a flock of wrens.

Usually I'm flooding and shouting, too. The churchyard begs to be run through, and flowers picked, and yew trees climbed.

But now might be a good time to find Lucy and Johanna. I have no liking for how we last parted, and it's easier to talk to them when there's something to keep their brothers and sisters busy.

Grown-ups start to appear as well. Some of them head home—it's past time for a meal—but many more linger on the steps. Mama Elly is catching up with some of the mamas she doesn't get to see often. I spot Papa with Henry at his side, and they're talking to Lucy's father.

Lucy's papa is one of the more important men in St Neots, mostly because he works with gold and therefore has dealings with people who can afford to own things made from gold. Whenever Johanna and I would play at Lucy's when we were small, he'd give a piece of marzipan to whichever of us could sit quietly the longest.

Papa has a hand on Henry's shoulder, but that's the only thing making him a part of the conversation.

Poor Henry. Stuck with the grown-ups since he wouldn't know any kid but me. Rabbits in snares look happier to be where they are.

I sigh, then weave through torrents of kids and head up the steps toward them.

It's not like I have to play with Henry. Just free him from all the tedious listening.

As I approach, Lucy's father tucks his thumbs in his belt in a satisfied way and says to Papa, "I expect you're quite glad to have the boy. Even if you're not, I certainly am. I won't have to hold my nose when your girl comes to visit mine."

Papa's neck reddens, but he only smiles tightly.

I can't help but smirk—Lucy's father pays so little attention to her that he doesn't even realize the last time I *came to visit* her, neither one of us had lost any milk teeth—before it occurs to me to wonder whether my own papa has realized how little time I spend with my friends.

"You'll make a fine apprentice, I'm sure," Lucy's papa says to Henry. "Come, we'll introduce you to the others."

Henry grins. All at once he looks grateful to fall in step with my papa and Lucy's, and they steer him toward a knot of men standing in the shade. There's a pause, then they all break out laughing and play-shoving Henry.

I can't move. Can't so much as pull in a breath.

All at once I don't feel like playing in the churchyard. I pad into the nave, fetch Mama Elly's stool, and put it in the wagon. Trudge shifts his weight, clearly ready to go back to his field. I pull some daisies from the verge and weave him a flower crown, but before I can settle it on his head, he takes a giant bite out of it.

I should be annoyed, but instead I giggle. It doesn't do to expect Trudge to be anything other than himself.

I thought the same was true of Papa, though. I never called myself an apprentice, or considered myself one. I was happy enough to simply dip and render and trim and sell.

I thought my papa was happy enough to have my willing hands and quick wit. It never occurred to me that he might want someone he could bring among his fellows and introduce around.

He couldn't do that with someone who would one day become young-womanly, even if she could dip and render as good as any boy.

It was going to happen sooner or later. You knew that, right?

No. I didn't. And apparently, I'm the only one who never saw it coming.

⇒ JULY ⇐

6

I AM no longer in charge of Trudge.

I got an earful when Papa noticed I've been neglecting the garden, so today after breakfast, he put the hoe and digger into my hands and marched me out there himself.

I tried to persuade him that the garden would be fine on its own, that I'd be of greater help in the rear yard, but he told me not to come back till I'd dumped two barrowloads of weeds on the midden.

All right, *fine*, it *is* hard to see the purslane under all of this ivy.

I'm hacking away with the hoe and wondering if I couldn't just bring Trudge here to eat the weeds clean out of the ground when a shadow falls over the row.

Henry, and he clears his throat and smiles. "Hey, Tick. Are you busy?"

It's on the tip of my tongue to snip at him. To oh-so-sweetly remind him how he took all my tasks away so *of course* I have nothing but time and this endless row of turnips to weed.

He's not the one who told me to collect barrowsful of weeds, though.

"Depends on what you mean by busy." I smile and drag my cuff across my forehead.

"Master Osbert wants me to go to the goldsmith's shop to collect some beeswax," Henry says, "and I thought perhaps you'd like to come along. Say hello to your friend. Linny?"

"Lucy," I reply, even though I'm not sure what sort of friends she and Johanna and I are now. The pair of them are so tightly knit together that there's not much room for someone who doesn't need their nose wiped or their bottom diapered.

But then I brighten, because if Henry is being sent for beeswax, it means the time has finally come to make Agnus Dei charms.

That means Papa finally has to let me help.

It takes a steady hand and keen sight to make charms. You must trim the cord to the exact length to make loops for hanging. You have to pour the right amount of melted wax onto the oiled canvas, and you must make sure you press the mold against the wax hard enough to imprint the picture, but not so hard that the wax squishes everywhere and makes an unsightly ridge.

That's before you consider the painting—cleaning and preparing the tiny brushes, mixing the paint, making each Agnus Dei the same as the last.

Henry might be a lot less hopeless at trimming fat and twisting wicks than he was when he got here, but wax charms are too much to entrust him with.

If a few candles are less than perfect, it won't be good, but there'll always be a buyer for a candle, however flawed. Agnus Dei charms, on the other hand—if they're not painted just right, people might not be as sure of the protection. They won't part with coin for them, and those charms are often the difference between a decent year at Stourbridge and a great one.

I stab my tools blade down in the dirt and hop-skip out of the furrows. I don't even scowl to think how Papa wouldn't so much as allow me the task of fetching beeswax. A task that takes no learning whatsoever.

Instead I smile at Henry and say, "Lead the way!"

Henry and I pick our way through the garden and step onto the road. He doesn't shove ahead or set a pace I can't match. We walk in silence at elbows with each other, and I hop-skip again, because it won't be long now before I'm back at my bright table where I belong, and there'll be cooled discs of wax all pressed with the little lamb and his banner, all the cord loops just so, ready for hanging from someone's belt or purse, or around their neck.

I'll trim each tiny brush perfectly. I'll mix the paints just like I've seen Papa do for years now, grain by grain, drop by drop of linseed oil.

I'll paint each charm with such patience and skill that Papa will come in after a long day of painstakingly teaching a perfectly nice but otherwise unqualified bumblefingers how to do things that I learned in a trice at half the years. He'll be holding one exhausted hand to his head and wondering why he ever thought an apprentice might be a good idea—and there I'll be.

At my bright table, my hair combed and my fingernails clean, with a perfect handful of Agnus Dei charms already pressed and painted, and more to come.

Papa will beg my pardon for inviting Henry here, and I'll agree to help him find a more suitable place for Henry to apprentice.

Papa will pull me into a tight hug and whisper how he can't do without me. He'll muss my hair like he did when I was small, and he'll hug me again, and even though I won't be invited to stand with Papa's friends after Mass, I'll be back up to my elbows in tallow and trailed by my furry shadows.

When we get to the high street, Henry falls behind a little, and it occurs to me—he doesn't know where the goldsmith lives.

It wasn't a simple kindness, him inviting me along. It had nothing to do with me at all.

I stop like Trudge, all feet all at once, sharp enough to send up a puff of dust. Then I spin on my heel and head back toward home. All but stomping.

There's a scuffle and a drum of footfalls, and Henry appears in front of me, quick-walking backward. "Tick? What's wrong?"

He sounds genuinely baffled, the clod, but right now I'm in no humor for excuses.

"You know what's wrong." I can't look at him. Kindness be hanged. "You're the proper apprentice. Find it yourself."

Henry looks pained. "Tick. Please. I . . . told your father I knew where the goldsmith's workshop is. That I *remembered*. Only I don't. So I need your help."

"You could have asked!" I snap, still walking, still clattering my feet hard against the road like Trudge when he's facing away from home.

"You're right. I should have." Henry runs both hands through his hair. "I just keep fouling things up. I wanted to do something right the first time. Even something as simple as fetching. Prove I have it in me to learn this trade well."

I start to preen a little—I like being right—but this isn't how I imagined being right would feel.

"But apparently, I can't," Henry mutters, "and your father's going to send me home."

He says it low and scared, like he knows something I don't.

I slow to a stop. I've been hoping for this moment for sennights now, but this is *definitely* not how I thought Henry leaving might feel.

"You gave chandling a good try. It's just not right for you." I edge a step nearer. "Besides, think how happy your parents will be to see you."

Henry blinks, but not quickly enough. Tears slip down his cheeks, and he scrubs them away, but not like he's trying to hide anything. More like he's so used to it that his wrist does it without his mind needing to guide the motion.

"That's the whole thing," he whispers. "I have to be good at this trade. I can't go home."

Henry is alone here. I'm the closest thing he's got to a friend, because whatever's bothering him, he doesn't feel like he can tell Papa, or Mama Elly, or he'd have done it by now.

"Why can't you go home?" I ask, trying not to sound as reluctant as I feel. "Is it because it's so far away? You made it here all right the first time."

Henry squints at me like I'm a dog he's not sure he should pet. At length he says, "That's because I didn't come from Norwich. I came from Cambridge."

"But Papa said you were from Norwich!"

"I was born there, near Holgate, but we've been living in Cambridge."

Now I'm frowning with my whole self. Cambridge is only a day's walk from here—two if you dawdle—and also the town you must travel through to get to the Stourbridge Fair. Henry's family must have *just* moved to Cambridge, because I can't imagine a world where Papa and I would rumble through those streets on our way to or from the fair and not visit his oldest friend.

Henry takes a deep breath. "The *we* is my sister and Mama. But not my father. He's still in Norwich. He's taken an apprentice so there's no place for me with him. No trade for me in Cambridge, either. When Da's message arrived saying your father was willing to take me on—it was a miracle."

"But . . ." I'm trying to make sense of this. "Your papa lives in a different place than your mama? How can that be . . . allowed?"

"Last fall, they decided to go their separate ways,"

Henry replies. "Before then, they fought all the time. Margaret and I, we'd hide in a corner and pull a blanket over our heads and say the paternoster with our fingers jammed in our ears so we didn't have to listen. Then one morning, they sat us down and explained that the two of us and Mama would be moving to Cambridge, into an empty house near Holy Trinity that her brother owns. Papa would stay in Norwich."

"They're still married, though, right?" I ask, mystified.

Henry nods. "There's no getting around that. But they wish they weren't, so they're going to live apart. After they decided it, though . . . it was like night and day. They were both smiling all the time. On the day we left Norwich, Papa loaded the wagon with his own hands and gave Mama some coin for the road. They even *hugged*."

I toe a line in the dust. It's like nothing I've ever heard before, and my family isn't what you'd call ordinary. Stepmothers are supposed to be jealous and terrible and dislike children they inherit by marriage. Mama Elly is the mama you want if you can't have the mama who birthed you.

"You can't tell your father, though." Henry leans close and lowers his voice, even though there's no one but us anywhere on the road. "I won't have him keeping me out of duty. Or worse, *pity*. I mean to learn this trade and learn it well."

"I'll try," I tell him, "but I'm a poor liar. Mama Elly says you can see every last thing I'm thinking on my face."

"You don't have to lie. Just keep it between us for now. Until I can tell him myself." Henry starts blinking quick again. "I'll owe you a favor."

I like the idea of Henry owing me a favor. So I nod.

"But what does your mother do in Cambridge?" I ask. "How does she keep herself, and you, and Margaret? She can't have a trade. Can she?"

"There are a lot of young men studying at the university who need bed and board," Henry replies. "Scholars pay well for three meals a day and a warm place to sleep. She does their laundry, too. When I left, there were four of them down in the undercroft, happy as larks to come up every morning to a good spread of fresh bread and butter before going to listen to the masters."

"Your mama lets young men she doesn't know live in her *house*?"

Henry lifts his brows. "I'm a young man you don't know, and Mama Elly lets me live in your house."

"Well." I fluster. "That's different. You're—" I'm about to say *you're a child*, but that sounds ruder than I intend. "You're here to learn a trade."

"And the scholars are in Cambridge to learn grammar and logic and rhetoric."

"I've been to Cambridge enough times to see scholars drunkenly wandering the alleys while shouting Latin poetry at one another in three-part rhyme. At *midday*." I fold my arms. "They're a troublesome lot. I wouldn't want them in my house."

"Some are. But there are more scholars than places to lodge, so Mama can pick and choose." Henry studies his feet. "Just like there are a lot of boys who want to learn a trade. Master Osbert can pick and choose. I need to give him a reason to choose me."

I frown. "Your father didn't tell you?"

"Tell me what?"

That our fathers were friends when they were young, and each promised to take the other's son into his trade. That my papa wouldn't dream of sending you home, not even if you end up the worst chandler for a day's ride in any direction.

Not when he got the better bargain—a proper apprentice who would never become young-womanly.

But I can't tell him that, so instead I say, "That Mama Elly would brain Papa with a kettle if he tried sending you on your way. She's more or less adopted you, so be ready for her to lick her thumb and wipe things off your face."

Henry laughs. "She's already done that. Twice."

"Come, let's go to the goldsmith's," I say. "Then you'll owe me two favors."

We're down the road another dozen steps before Henry clears his throat. "Thank you, Tick."

"What for? I didn't do much but listen."

"Sometimes," he says, quiet and sidelong, "listening is a lot."

7

HENRY LOOKS incredulous when I stop in front of the goldsmith's workshop, like maybe I'm playing a joke on him.

Not many other buildings take up two plots on the high street, and none but this one has four big windows, each with a sturdy set of red shutters studded with tiny gilded crosses, and limewash so new it almost hurts your eyes.

The door is carved with leaves and flowers and polished to a shine, and Henry's knuckles hesitate over it.

The shutters are propped open, though, and both of us watch Lucy's brother Hodge working the bellows by the hearth. He's three years older than us, but he hasn't changed a diaper or washed a dish since Lucy got big enough to do it.

When he sees me, Hodge lifts his brow in the most unpleasant smirk I've seen in some time.

I'm used to mutters. I'm used to people keeping plenty clear of me. But most folks understand that there's nothing to be done about the smell of our yard, or the road out front, or my gown, or sometimes my hair.

They might stay away, but they're not *mean* about it.

I turn to Henry. "Right. I didn't come all this way to put up with Hodge. I'm through to the garden to find Lucy. See you at home."

Henry's eyes go big. "You—you're not going to stay?"

"Why? Lucy won't be in the workshop."

When he bites his lip, I muffle a sigh, then rap at the door sharp and confident. For all that Henry's supposed to be the proper apprentice, he has so very much to learn.

When someone inside calls for us to enter, I put my shoulder against the door and push in like it's my own house.

Lucy's papa looks up from his long, weathered worktable. He is not cuddly and tumbly like Johanna's father, and he has very specific thoughts on little girls in his workshop, especially when the fire's stoked and there's liquid gold in the crucible, and he is not shy about sharing those thoughts in a louder voice than you'd think a white-haired spindle of a man would have.

I may be a child, but I am not a little girl.

"Good morning," I say with my nicest smile. "Have you the beeswax?"

He frowns. "The apprentice lad isn't here?"

I try very hard not to bristle, because if I'm rude to the goldsmith, he'll be sure to tell my papa. Instead I push the door open wider so he can see Henry. "We've both come. I'm helping him learn his tasks."

Henry steps into the room beside me. He lifts a hand in a shy greeting.

Lucy's papa glances between us once, twice, then a grin comes over his face like the Almighty just whispered a secret in his ear. "Helping, eh? Perhaps a little kissing along the way?"

"What? *No!*" I leap apart from Henry as if he licked me. "I am a *child* and besides that, I have no interest in courting, and even if I did, I'd have no interest in *him*."

Next to me, Henry is turning scarlet, and I'm realizing how it might have been what I meant but I could have put it a lot kindlier. So I start babbling, "That is. Nothing against him. Just. There's no *courting* here."

"Definitely not," Henry adds, with enough force that it can't help but sting even though I'm glad to hear it.

"He wouldn't know you keep the wax on a high shelf, or that Father Leo should bless it." I'm indignant now, snapping the words like frozen twigs. I turn to

Henry and add, "Proper Agnus Dei charms are made of wax from melted-down candles that were used to celebrate Easter, but as long as the wax has been blessed, Papa figures the Almighty will look kindly on whoever's carrying it."

Lucy's papa goes *pshhh-pshhh*. "I meant nothing by it, of course. Soon enough you'll change your mind." He winks knowingly, and I want badly to kick him hard in the shins. "All girls do, and at least one father can't wait for that day to come."

I'm about to inform him that *my* father doesn't—but then I reckon how I don't know whether that's true. Since Henry took my place, Papa and I haven't traded above five words that weren't *Is there more bread?* and *Tick, dear one, can you please move out of the way?*

Then there was Mama Elly's growing-up talk. All that business about courting, as if I'd shown a thimbleful of interest in it.

"How goes the chandling?" Lucy's papa is asking, and I'm about to tell him how painfully far behind we are when I realize he's talking to Henry.

Henry launches into a diverse array of falsehoods in which he insists that fifty pounds of candles have already been trimmed, dipped, and coated in the varnish that helps them burn steadily, packed away for the fair nice and tidy.

There's no way that can be true, though. That would mean Papa isn't behind on candlemaking at all, that Henry really is picking things up quickly and there truly will be plenty of candles of all grades and sizes to sell at the fair.

"Your sweetheart was right about the wax." Lucy's papa gestures to the high shelf where bricks of beeswax form a golden wall. "Help yourself to one. Osbert has already arranged for payment."

Henry nods politely, even though his cheeks are burning. He pushes a stool over and starts to climb. I have to turn away from the goldsmith before I say something I'll want back, and that's when I notice the cat crouched under a table beneath the window. Out of habit I reach a hand toward her. She's black with a white belly, and she pushes her nose deeply into my hem and rubs.

Hodge cackles and makes a show of holding his nose. I ignore him and kneel to better rub the cat's ears, and when I do, I notice a little glint in the dust behind a bag of sawdust. Lucy's scoundrel of a brother is still making a show of preventing the smell of me getting into his nose, so he doesn't see me whisk the glinty thing into my palm and turn toward the door where he can't see.

Even once I've brushed off the dust, I'm not sure what it is. It's roundish like the Agnus Dei mold, but smaller, the size of two thumbs together, and the picture is raised instead of carved in.

I tip the glinty thing toward the light. The picture is a creature of some sort—four paws, a tail—and the kind of stance that makes me think of Big Gray. There's a loop at the top, which makes me think it's meant to be worn, but no ribbon or cord or fastener.

Lucy's papa is not the sort of person to carelessly mislay something glinty. It might be lost, and I should—

Without warning, there's a flutter of footfalls outside, then the door pushes wider and smacks me right in the knees. Lucy steps through the door with a basket on her arm that smells like fresh pease bread and yellow cheese. She stops when she sees me, baffled, before her eyes go to the glinty in my hands.

I pull a fist around it, press it against my chest.

Lucy stands in the doorway, in shadow. I clutch the glinty tighter. I'm caught, and there's no way to explain this.

Especially not to Lucy.

Her papa breaks the stillness with a mighty sigh. "What have I told you about barging in like this? And look at the *state* of you!"

Lucy scrambles to pull a veil over her wild, flyaway hair and straightens her wilting apron. Then she curtsies. She *curtsies*, just like her papa is the prior, or the bailiff, or a particularly thunderous matron who has no patience for untidiness.

"Beg pardon, Father," she murmurs. "Mama needs a kettle lifted. She said to send Hodge or come yourself."

I'm not sure what shocks me most—how Lucy's unapologetic fishwife voice quiets to a sweet, demure mumble, or how she tends to her appearance as if she cares a lick for it, or how she calls her papa *Father*, when the goldsmith has always been a papa just like mine.

"Every small thing must always be a fuss with you, mustn't it? Think how wonderfully quiet the house will be when you marry." The goldsmith turns to his son. "Hodge, you don't have a friend who'd take her right now, do you?"

There's playfulness in it, but something else, too.

"Not unless she comes with a muzzle for her dowry," Hodge drawls, grinning wide and lazy like a dog in the sun.

Lucy's papa turns to Henry with a kind of smile that lets you in on a joke that isn't meant to be funny to everyone. "I understand your father is a tanner. Any chance he can make a muzzle for my girl?"

Lucy blinks rapidly.

Hodge cackles.

Henry steps off the stool. He's holding a brick of beeswax in both hands, and he deliberately lands with both feet, *thump*. Hodge and his papa both turn to look at him instead of Lucy, and in that moment I could hug him.

Lucy doesn't waste the gift. She darts out of the workshop, pulling her veil tighter as she goes.

"Hodge, go help your mother," the goldsmith says, as if we'd all just been discussing the weather. He nods to Henry and asks, "Will that brick do?"

"Yes, thank you." Henry dips his chin, polite, and turns to hold the door open for me.

As we step into the road, we hear a murmured chuckle of *Not courting, my hairy bum!*

Henry looks at me. I look at him.

"We are *friends*," he says, like he's drawing a line, and I nod so hard it makes my teeth clench, even though it hasn't been long since I thought of him more as a headache than anything else. The sting of it reminds me that I'm still holding tight to the glinty I found on the floor.

I should return it. I know I should, but I sincerely believe I will do violence to Sir Hairy Bum if I have to endure that smirk one moment longer.

"So you have time for friends now, do you?" Lucy lingers near the gutter. She's pushed her veil back, and the sun makes a halo on her shiny hair.

I'm stung. Lucy's the last person who should be throwing stones. Not with that embroidery on her apron that matches Johanna's.

"Come now, that's unkind," I reply, because it's something Mama Elly says all the time and it always makes me start guessing where I've stepped in it. "Besides, I came all this way just to say hello."

Lucy cuts a glance at Henry. "Yes, I imagine you have all kinds of time on your hands these days. You said this boy wouldn't be staying, and yet he remains. Now you know how it feels to have someone you love abandon you just because they got a better offer."

It's like she doesn't remember all the times she and Johanna stood together at Mass when I was trapped at the back, near the open door where the strong reek of tallow could be bettered by fresh air. All the times she crossed the road when she saw me coming just to keep from smelling me.

"We should be getting back," Henry says into the silence, holding up the brick of beeswax.

"Then go," Lucy says in a no-nonsense voice, and she moves a gaze over us both like she already knows what I'm going to do, and if there's one thing Lucy loves more than anything, it's being right.

I hesitate. Wroth as I am. *Trembling* as I am.

Because it's also true that I never liked holding a baby brother or sister when it was my turn. I had little patience for babble and less for tantrums. When it was just the three of us, we could play elaborate games of make-believe that took up whole afternoons. With younger kids, it was nothing but tag, and even that they couldn't play for half a moment without forgetting they were it and chasing a butterfly.

It's also true that I was the one who was too busy to play every time one of them turned up at the door.

Not long ago, Lucy invited me to spend the afternoon with her and Johanna at the mill. I was the one who turned her down before the spoons were even washed.

I can't miss out on making wax charms. I've been waiting for years for the chance, and Papa promised the task to me.

But Henry can't make the charms by himself. He doesn't know how, and Papa won't be able to teach him to mix pigments or paint the charms correctly, not given his poor eyesight. Mama Elly has no interest in such things.

That leaves only me.

Without me there won't be any charms, and charms always sell briskly at the Stourbridge Fair, being so many travelers there and all.

They will have to wait for me.

I turn to Henry. "You go ahead, all right? I'll catch up."

"Are you sure?" he asks.

I'm not, but I just say, "Don't forget to go by the church to get the wax blessed."

Lucy and I watch Henry disappear down the high street toward St Mary's. Then I meet her eye steady on.

"You were right. Henry is my father's new apprentice." It stings to say it aloud. "I don't get to help with candlemaking anymore. You were right, and it happened just like you said."

Lucy drops her hostile stance. She peers at me as if she's listening, but begrudgingly. Like she's glad she's right, and glad I confessed as much, but not glad it's true.

"I haven't been a good friend of late. To you and Johanna both."

"For a long while now." Lucy says it matter-of-fact, but there's a turn of hurt down deep. "Ever since you started helping your father and didn't have time for us anymore. It's been years now. *Years.*"

"I just . . ." I look at my hands, the backs covered with tiny, darkened speckles of burn where the tallow splattered. "I just wanted to do something that matters."

Lucy frowns. "How can you believe minding children doesn't matter? How do you think any of us turn out to be decent people if there's not someone around who cares enough to make sure we get that way? To make sure you know how to share? To beg someone's pardon if you wrong them? To give someone a hug if they're upset?"

My cheeks burn. "They're not my brothers and sisters, though."

"All the more reason," she replies. "It's one thing if I care about them. I *have* to. But when someone else cares who has no blood reason to? It tells them that they matter to more than just their family. They matter to everyone."

Mama Elly has no blood reason to care about me, but she swept very small Tick into her arms and has never let go, even when I am not at my best.

"You and Johanna are so close," I say to my feet. "You have the little ones in common. You've shared so much, and I . . ."

"Always smelled like a butcher shop in August," Lucy says, in a way she likely means to be teasing but just comes out unkind. Then she adds, "You don't today, though."

I look down at myself. At my gown that's somewhat dusty but without a single tallow spatter. This is what my father wants for me. What Mama Elly wants, too. *A girl should have friends.*

I mumble something about aprons. Something about tallow and cats and where my family stands at Mass.

"I thought you were happy to be rid of us, but maybe that wasn't true." Lucy bumps her shoulder into mine. "I'm late meeting Jo at the well. We're taking the kids to see what berries we can find. I suppose I'll see you on Sunday?"

I love the smell of beeswax. I love how every brick is its own color, no two alike, as if the bees made each one special for a certain purpose.

I've been waiting for years to make Agnus Dei charms all on my own. But I can wait a little longer.

I bump Lucy back and say, "Maybe I can come with you."

8

THE FIRST THING I do is repeat my apology to Johanna. I'm hardly done speaking before she hugs me and says how *she's* the one who's sorry.

"I had no idea you felt left out, Tick," she tells me. "If you like, I'll ask Mama for some green floss so you can embroider your apron to match ours."

I would, and I tell her so. It's likely going to take a great deal more to make the three of us like we were, but this is a good place to start.

We head for the millpond. No one yells *stench* or holds their nose. The little kids are too happy to have a meadow to run through and a creek to splash in. Lucy warns them to stay within sight of the mill or there will be consequences, while Johanna promises them a treat if they do as they're told.

I've missed my friends.

Once the kids scatter, the three of us lie belly down on the creek bank. The grass is cool and there's a dapple of shade, and best of all, we have the creek to look at instead of one another.

If I had a penny for every day we spent like this when we were smaller, I'd have a sack I couldn't lift.

It's different now, though, in a way I'm not sure I can name.

It's been days and days since Papa has mussed my hair or handed me a tool or asked me to stir or fetch something. Too long since we talked about anything beyond why the stew was cold.

Lucy is not round in her womanly places like Johanna. Put her in a tunic and hose and she'd look like a boy.

Yet her papa has decided she's done enough growing up that he can suggest without much hint of jest that she ought to be married.

Not her papa. *Father.*

I want to say something to Lucy about what happened at the workshop. How her father spoke to her, *of* her, how he got Hodge to go along and how he tried to pull Henry in, just because they were boys.

It's almost like I want to tell her I'm sorry, even though I did nothing wrong. Sorry it happened, maybe. Sorry I was there to *see* it happen.

Sorry any of us have to grow up, if this is what growing up means.

I don't, though. Instead I tell Johanna, "Your Agnus Dei will be ready soon. I'm going to be starting them tomorrow probably."

She squeals and claps like a little kid shown honey cake, and right there I promise myself that I'll paint her charm last, so it's the very best of what I can do.

"You want one, too?" I ask Lucy. When she hitches a shoulder, *I don't care*, we grow quiet again. It's almost like after so long we don't share much anymore.

I want us to share things again. I want to tell them everything that's been going on. How much it hurts that Papa's given all my tasks to Henry, how determined I am to prove to Papa that I'm just as good as any boy apprentice, even if he can't show me around to his friends the same way.

But that will split open wounds that are just starting to mend.

So I reach into my apron pouch, show them the glinty, and ask, "What do you think this is?"

"It's a kitty!" Johanna reaches for it eagerly, and I let her take it. As she examines the object, I realize she's right—the picture is definitely some sort of cat, although it's hulking and shaggy.

"I thought that's what I saw you with." Lucy is

smiling in that thorny way of hers, and I go tense until she cackles, "*Father* has torn the shop apart for that brooch for months now. He made it special for a master in Cambridge. It's meant to be the lion of St Mark."

"Oh! Then I'm glad I found it." I try for a smile and add, "Perhaps returning it will put you in his good graces."

Lucy scowls. "I'm in no hurry to help *Father*. He can whistle for his supper."

"That's a lot of gold to whistle for," Johanna says, her eyes big and scared. "If you don't want to hand it along yourself, your mama could do it, right?"

"It's only gilded. Gold over wood. Adam did the carving. It took him an age, but it's pretty good for someone who's only eight, don't you think?" Lucy grins at me. "He said he made the likeness after one of the cats who live in Trudge's byre. The big one that looks like a church bell."

"Still." Johanna lifts her brows at Lucy. "It must be of value or your father wouldn't be so anxious to get it back."

"*Father* can have it back when he stops being awful to me." Lucy plucks the brooch out of Johanna's hand and drops it into mine. "But that's going to be never, so you keep it, Tick. It's your cat in the image, and besides, it would serve *Father* right."

"Big Gray's not mine," I reply quickly, like this is the

most important thing, but then I realize what Lucy is saying, what she'd have me do.

Because I'm finding it hard to disagree. It *would* serve Sir Hairy Bum right.

But if my papa found out, he'd be furious.

"I'll keep it for now," I reply, slow and careful. "Until you want it back. All right?"

Lucy makes a brushing-away motion, *piff-piff*, like she's never going to want it back.

The brooch feels heavy and cold on my palm. Like how I always imagined gold would feel. I close my hand around it.

Knowing that Adam thinks Big Gray is akin to the lion of St Mark makes me like the boy a little more.

We spend the afternoon in the field. There are three tantrums and a squabble over the last piece of cheese, and I'd surely rather be trimming fat or even mixing varnish, but if I want us to share things again, I have to meet my friends where they are.

No one mutters or even whispers *stench*. Johanna even shoulder-bumps me playfully as she drops Waleran in my arms.

Late in the afternoon, we part ways. Lucy waves, and Johanna mentions at least thrice how they're often here since their brothers and sisters love the millpond so much.

This time I don't hesitate at all. "I can't promise to come every day, but I'll be here when I can."

I smile the whole walk home. I smile because I *should* have friends, same as Papa, same as anyone who does work. I smile because there's a brooch in my apron pouch that Lucy trusts me to hold for her, that will keep her scoundrel of a father spinning, because who tells a *child* that she should be courting?

A scoundrel, that's who.

I'm smiling as I come into the yard, empty of cats now that there's no meat scraps in the offing, and I actually miss them and the way they pursue what they want regardless of what others think.

Smiling as I come through the workshop, even though the whole place smells like fresh tallow and the big rack is draped with dozens of drying candles, hanging in pairs with one long wick between them.

Smiling as I hug Mama Elly standing at the kettle on my way through the kitchen to the hall.

But when I move into the hall, I stop short. I stop smiling. I might stop breathing.

Henry is sitting at my bright table. The window is open to catch the last of the falling daylight, and lined up before him, around him, are dozens upon dozens of wax discs.

They can't be Agnus Dei charms. They *can't* be.

His back is to me, but on the floor at his feet is the wooden carryall where we keep the pigments and oils, the tiny reeds, the penknife, the quills.

There's nothing else they can be.

I'm across the room in four strides. My hands are fists now, my teeth grinding. Henry looks up, and his face is open and innocent, the blackguard. He pauses in his crushing of some red ocher with Papa's good soapstone mortar and pestle.

"What—?" I choke on my rage and stab a hand helplessly at the wax discs stretching across the table, unpainted, unvarnished, helpless and ugly, snails without their shells. "What are you *doing*?"

"Ah." Henry frowns, holds up the pestle. "Smashing things?"

I pull in a long, long breath. Push it out so hard it echoes through my nose. Again, because it's the only thing keeping tears from my eyes.

Papa steps breezily into the room. He's carrying the heavy wooden serving tray that's hard for Mama Elly to handle, and he sets it on the trestle board with a flourish. He sees me and smiles. "There's my Tick! Can you lay the table for us?"

I round on him. Nearly blind with fury. "Making charms was to be my job, Papa. You promised me. You *promised*!"

Papa frowns, baffled. "You still want to do that?"

"Of course I do!" I snap. "Haven't you been *listening*? I've talked about little else all winter and most of spring!"

"Oh. Well." Papa scratches his beard. "Henry here brought the beeswax, so we got it melted and poured and stamped in a trice. Lad's a quick learner!"

Henry scrunches his neck into his collar like a dog when you smack it on the nose.

"I suppose you can show him how to mix the paint," Papa goes on, like he didn't just admit that he hadn't, in truth, been listening. "I'd do it myself, but there are still plenty of candles to dip before dark."

"That's not why, and we both know it!" It's out of my mouth before I can bite it back.

Papa's eyes get big. Then they narrow. "Scholastica. That's enough."

He glances quick and furtive toward Henry, and in that moment I realize that he hasn't said a word to his proper apprentice about his failing eyesight.

"Well. Perhaps I won't have time. All those growing things that need my attention." I square up like Trudge when he's had enough pulling for one day. "I suppose *you'll* have to show him. After all, Henry deserves to be taught the trade from a master."

The hall goes still. I go still. Papa isn't the sort of

man who raises his hand in anger, but I'm glad I'm across the room from him.

He levels a finger at me. "To bed with you. No supper."

I turn without a word. Up the ladder I go, and I drop onto my bed and fold my arms over my middle and breathe.

It was bad enough, being banished to the garden. Bad enough to watch Henry make a hash of the simplest things, win the cats so easily.

When someone breaks a promise, clear-eyed, with intent—that's hard to bear.

After a while Henry's head appears through the hole in the floor. "Mama Elly says to come down to supper."

I don't want to. Even though the pottage smells heavenly. Even though Mama Elly clearly won the day when it comes to my eating it.

"I didn't know about the wax charms," he adds quietly.

I sigh, then slide off my bed and follow Henry down the ladder. The table is laid with our wooden plates and mugs, with the serving dish of what now must be lukewarm pottage.

Papa is at his place at the head of the trestle board, and Henry sits on the bench at his right hand. He still blocks the sight of my bright table, but right now I don't mind as much.

I slide into my space on the bench at Papa's left. It's hard not to feel how angry Papa still is about what I said. It drifts off him like the smell of tallow. The *stink* of it.

It was a low blow, flinging Papa's eyesight back at him like I did. He feels shame enough already, and that's before all the work it takes to keep people in St Neots from finding out.

But it was a low blow, too, Papa expecting me to show Henry how to take away yet another task, one I've been waiting years to be trusted with.

Only maybe I can't afford Papa being angry. He'll spend the whole evening talking with Henry about why wool is curly and whether roses could ever bloom in winter. He won't miss me at all.

So I clear my throat and say, "Papa, I would like to beg your pardon for speaking so discourteously. I . . ."

I was so disappointed.

I couldn't believe you broke your promise.

I am losing you.

"I was upset," I finally manage, "and I could have chosen my words better."

Mama Elly comes in with a basket of bread, her brace scraping the floor, and she gives Papa such a fierce look that he puts down his spoon and looks right at me for the first time in a long while.

"You surely could have, Tick," he says. "You have

my pardon, but from now on, there'll be no more such rudeness."

Then he reaches for the pitcher and pours himself some ale.

"Give our child a hug," Mama Elly scolds. She's holding the bread, not putting it on the table, as if she intends to keep it from him until he does what she bids him.

Henry's whole attention is on his lap. His cheeks are bright red, as if he's the one who's embarrassed here, and it takes a moment for me to realize that grown-ups arguing must be hard for him to hear, given what befell his parents.

Papa seems to crack a little. He smiles in his old way and pushes the bench back so he can open his arms properly.

Only I'm the one still frozen. Mama Elly had to tell him to give me a hug, and sure enough he's doing just that, but moments ago he was ready to simply go on with supper.

All at once I don't want a hug. I want to flounce out of the room so he'll be left with empty arms and perhaps a whisper of what I feel right now.

I can't, though. If my hugs are numbered, I want every last one of them.

So I walk around the table and put my arms around

Papa's shoulders. He holds me tight and I breathe in the smell of him, old tallow and woodsmoke and the smallest whiff of armpit sweat.

"There," says Mama Elly. "That's better, don't you think?"

No one replies, so I sit back down, my footsteps echoing.

Mama Elly tries to start a conversation, asking me if Johanna's mama has had the baby yet, asking Henry if he's got any hand for mending wicker fish traps, but mostly we shovel in pottage while she fills the air with cheerful chatter.

Well. Papa and Henry shovel. I have to force down bite after bite, when behind Henry on my bright table I can see the pale outline of dozens of wax charms, each one its own broken promise.

After supper, I scrub the plates and mugs and set them on their shelf to dry. I take my ease with it. All this time spent washing is time I'm not mixing paints, which means time Henry can't be working on the charms.

I want Papa to really think about how much he needs me. I want him to really feel my absence.

Besides, it's good to scrub. It gives me a place to put my wrothfulness.

Mayhap I should simply refuse to mix the paints. Put my nose in the air and take myself off to bed in a

J. ANDERSON COATS

huff. Force Papa to admit to Henry that the world is just smears of color to him.

But that'll mean there won't be any Agnus Dei charms to sell at the fair, and that could very well lead to empty bellies in winter.

Someone will have to show Henry how to paint an Agnus Dei, and there's no one but me who can do it. I'm in a position to ask for something, and there's no reason for Papa to say me nay.

Once the last plate is clean, I dry my hands on a rag and head into the hall. Now is not the time to hold a grudge. Anyone can melt wax and pour it into discs on oiled canvas. The *real* work is in the painting.

Henry is sitting at the bright table, and Papa stands beside it, gesturing down at something.

". . . just a dab at a time," Papa is saying as I approach, and he hands Henry a flat tool with a groove at the end. A tool I helped him make years ago to aid with the measuring of tiny amounts of precious pigments.

Henry is gently cradling half an eggshell in his palm. With the scoop tool, he dips a thumbnail's worth of egg white out of an oyster shell at the top corner of the table.

"That's just right," Papa says. "Tick can help you from here. It's not as hard as she wants to make it. You're a bright lad. You'll pick it up quick."

Papa turns and nearly bumps into me. I look up at

him, up and up, and it should be me at the bright table mixing pigments and getting ready to paint charms. It should be the two of us like it's always been, side by side in the purple twilight, wondering about the world.

That always felt like a promise.

"So. Ah." I cast around for something to hold him here. Even though I'm angry. "The ocher. It's so red. I wonder how it got that way. And why the yellow ocher is yellow, if it came out of the same ground."

Papa puts a hand to his bristly chin. Like he did when I was five, seven, ten, and asked the kind of question he could really put some thought into. When he'd give me an answer the same as he'd give one of his fellows.

Then he turns to Henry and says, "What do you think, son?"

Henry blinks. He looks flattered to be asked, and he launches into supposings about the differences in the textures of earth that might be interesting if my whole insides weren't churning.

But he must see the look about me, because he trails off, clears his throat, and shakes the slither of egg white off the spoon tool into the eggshell he's holding.

"That's not how you do it," I say, even though it's *exactly* how you do it.

Papa looks from Henry to me, then sighs as if I'm the one in the wrong.

"No one meddles like a woman," Papa mutters, and I go cold to the marrow because it wasn't meant for me to hear and that means it's something he believes but doesn't want me to know about.

That he doesn't agree with Mama Elly that I'm a child. That I might not have done all my growing up, but I'm now someone who meddles instead of someone who helps.

"This is why you're to keep your distance," Papa says to me. "Henry is never going to learn if no one lets him, and right now you're half an eyeblink from snatching the tools away and doing the measuring for him."

"I *might* not be," I grumble, but to prove he's wrong and I had no intention whatsoever of doing just that, I pick up another half eggshell and turn to Henry. "Right. You measure pigment in grains. First you crush it, which you've already done . . . Papa, don't you have work to do in the yard?"

Papa stands over me, arms folded. "I always have work, pet."

My ears burn. He doesn't trust me. Me, who he once left in the yard alone hour upon hour to dip the candles steady and even in the deep trough. Who singlehandedly kept up the fire, trimmed fat, fed the cats, twisted wicks, and fetched water for Mama Elly in the meantime.

I talk Henry through the mixing of two colors, red

ocher in his eggshell and green earth in mine. It's what a chandler would do, so that's what I do.

"Now it's time for the painting," I say, and I can't keep the delight from my voice as I reach for a plain wax Agnus Dei from the bright table. "You'll want to choose a nice bendy reed, then trim it—"

"Henry can take it from here." Papa grips my elbow and pulls me gently away from the table. "Go help Mama Elly take in the washing."

I hesitate. Mama Elly doesn't like anyone helping her unless she asks, and Papa has been standing here by the bright table the whole time and couldn't know her mind.

"I ought to help Henry with the painting," I reply. "He won't know how to paint an Agnus Dei. I'm the one who has to show him. It's one thing if a candle or two is lopsided, but an Agnus Dei has to be *right*."

Papa lifts his brows, and I hasten to add, "That wasn't rude. It's *true*."

"Off you go, Scholastica," he replies, his smile a thin line.

I take my time settling the eggshell of paint into Papa's outstretched palm. Giving him one last chance to make this right.

When he doesn't, I leave without another word.

9

MAMA ELLY is delighted to have help with the laundry. When it's all in the basket, she sends me to the stream for one last bucket of water before night closes in completely.

Being outside as the sun sinks into purples and blues is usually my favorite part of summer, and I try to enjoy the cool air on my face, the soft dirt beneath my feet.

When I get back, I leave the water in the kitchen and head right for the bright table, where I spot Henry, bent over his work once again.

That can't be right, though. Henry wouldn't know what to do.

I pad across the room and peek over his shoulder. The eggshells of paint are balanced on a rag to keep them steady and upright. In his left hand is a half-painted Agnus Dei, and in his right is a reed with a tip that's trimmed at too shallow an angle.

The lamb should be white, but instead he's covered with a two-color thumb smudge. The banner, which should be delicately crossed with red, is dripping toward the ground below and pooling like a slaughter on grass that looks more like a river.

Henry glances up at me. His smile is rueful. "This is harder than it looks. But I think I'm getting it."

My heart is beating in great, red throbs. We can't sell these at the fair. No traveler will put silver down for such poor work, and worse, Papa's reputation will be in tatters.

"How—how do you—are you making this up as you go?" I ask, and it's all I can do to make it a real question and not a gasp of pure discourtesy.

Henry points to a small square of linen at his elbow. On it sits an Agnus Dei, an old one, the colors faded and the wax shiny with years of thumbs rubbing it in prayer. It has a cord loop at the top, frayed by time, and strung through the loop is a length of ribbon woven in a faint yellow pattern.

"But where did it come from?" I ask, genuinely baffled. "We've never left Stourbridge with a single charm unsold."

"Master Osbert wouldn't say," Henry replies, "but I think it might have been your mother's."

I start to correct him, that Mama Elly has no interest in wax charms, but then I pull in a sharp breath and I am out the front door and around to the rear yard where Papa is trying to pry open one of the candle molds.

"It was hers, wasn't it?" My voice is a rasp.

Papa says nothing, and that's all the reply I need. My mother had an Agnus Dei, and my father never thought to show it to me. Never thought to let me know he had it tucked away in a linen cloth, away from me, her only child.

Instead he handed it to Henry as if it were any other charm, as if its only good was in the colors he could copy.

One more thing that Papa shared with Henry without a thought for how it might hurt me.

Mama Elly finds me hiding in Trudge's byre, facedown in the straw. I hear the scrape of her brace moving across the hard-baked yard well before she gets here, and I feel a plummet of guilt because I know how hard it is for her to walk outside where the ground is uneven.

She's going to want to know what's wrong, and I can't tell her about the Agnus Dei. Mama Elly gets downcast when anyone brings up my first mother, like she's going to rise from the grave and snatch me back. Like Mama Elly is a distant second best, when she's all the mama I've ever known and I love her to bits.

I wish that were the worst of it.

There's a faint groan and a heavy shape lands in the straw next to me, then a gentle hand on my back.

"Why'd he break his promise?" I murmur.

"Your papa just wants you to have a happy life. The kind your friends are going to have."

"But why doesn't he want me to have the kind of happy life that *I* want to have?" I sit up and brush straw from my hair. "Why don't *you*?"

"You're thinking about what makes you happy right now," Mama Elly replies. "Chances are very good that's going to change sooner than any of us know."

I muffle a groan. "We already had the growing-up talk, remember? If a boy doesn't like the way I smell, that's his concern, not mine."

"It's not just a matter of smell," she tells me. "Your father is starting to see himself through the eyes of others."

"That's *good*, though," I argue. "They're seeing a man who's entrusting his only daughter with important work and teaching her everything she might want to know about chandling."

Mama Elly shakes her head. "They were seeing a man

so miserly that he wouldn't even take an apprentice to spare his only daughter being spattered with tallow so thick that every cat in two shires loves her more than any decent boy ever will."

"But I'm a *child*," I remind her. "I have no need of boys, decent or otherwise, and what's wrong with cats in two shires loving me?"

"They were seeing the kind of father who can't provide for his family," she says quietly, "and your papa doesn't like being that man."

"But nothing has changed!" I protest. "I've been making candles at his side for years now."

Mama Elly glides a kind hand over my cheek. "Oh, my lamb. You are the one who'll soon be changing."

I fall backward into the straw and stare at the roof thatch. Mama Elly can't help but see the good in what Papa thinks to do. Her own papa had very little time for a daughter he saw as a burden, so she spun and fetched and carried and hobbled her braced leg raw to win his love, only it never worked.

Mama Elly is not going to take my side.

She might even have been the one who whispered in Papa's ear in the first place, suggesting it was time for him to send for his friend's son to become his apprentice, to carry out the promise he made in boyhood.

Mama Elly lures me back into the house with the

offer of a hot tisane with mint and lemon balm and a little drip of honey. As she pours the steaming water, she asks if I want to talk more, but I shake my head and she leaves me in peace.

I sit on the kitchen hearth bench, the mug warm in my hands, comforting like a hug. Through the doorway, I can hear Papa and Henry talking about tomorrow's work.

This time last year, that was me at Papa's side, nodding along with his plans, suggesting my own. The two of us together. I wish I'd have known to treasure those moments.

"We'll try to settle another six pounds of candles," Papa is saying, "and after supper, you can keep on with the charms in what's left of the daylight."

"Very well, but have a look at what I've done so far," Henry replies. "It's not much like the one you said I'm to copy, and Tick told me you rely on the silver these bring at the fair."

"You're doing fine work, son," Papa says firmly. "Don't let *anyone* tell you otherwise."

I bring my mug down with a thump.

Papa can't see Henry's work well enough to know how poor it is. Henry is never going to ask me to help because he doesn't know just how bumbling the paintwork truly is.

I can't let this happen. We need every coin, especially if we're not going to have as many candles as we should.

I push away from the table, but that's as far as I get.

Papa will never believe me if I try to tell him. He'll be convinced that I'm *meddling*.

Maybe I can tell Henry, though. Only this morning he said we were friends, and if there's one thing I've learned about losing friends, it happens when you figure you know what they're thinking instead of just asking.

Before long, Henry and I are in the loft, each of us settling into bed. I'm glad for the dim, because saying this is going to be hard enough.

"Look, about your painting." I sigh. "I don't mean to be discourteous, but it's not very good."

Henry frowns. "But Master Osbert said it was fine."

Papa has gone to considerable lengths to keep his failing eyesight a secret in St Neots. Henry's sure to learn of it sooner or later, but if he finds out from me, Papa will be furious.

"It's not," I say simply. "Your hand is smeary and shaky. No one's going to buy a charm with such unsteady work. I'm sorry."

Henry goes quiet. At first I'm sure he's going to snap at me and tell me to mind my business, or accuse me of trying to take over his tasks because I'm envious.

Instead he starts weeping into his sleeve, and in that

moment I remember how worried he is that Papa will dismiss him for incompetence, that he can't lose this position because he has nowhere to go.

Henry might not do everything as quickly as I do. He certainly doesn't do it as well.

But he never has to be told anything twice. He doesn't daydream or cut corners.

He's getting better every day.

I slide off my bed and go sit next to him on his pallet. I mean it as a kindness, but it makes him scrub his eyes and pull in a heaving breath and master himself.

"This is terrible," Henry murmurs. "If your father can't even tell me truly how my work is, that must mean he can't be bothered to teach me properly. He *is* only keeping me out of pity."

"Better to ask and know the truth, even if it's hard." I glance at Henry sidelong, and even though the words are like chewing old straw, I add, "But if it makes you feel better, I don't think it's true. I think Papa values your work considerably."

Henry nods. He scrubs his cuff over his eyes again.

"I could help you with the painting," I say softly. "Papa doesn't have to know."

That makes Henry stiffen. "Your father's right, though. I'll never learn if I don't work at it."

"No one's saying I'd be doing it for you. Just helping."

"I've still got a while before the fair," Henry replies. "I want to try on my own. The paint wipes off easily when it's still wet. If Agnus Dei charms really are worth their weight in silver, I need to be able to paint one perfectly in my sleep."

I jump to my feet. I go back to my own bed. I don't quite stomp, but it's close.

"If my work still isn't good enough by September, you can help, all right?" Henry's voice comes through the dark like an apology, like a plea. Like how Johanna promises the little kids a treat if they behave.

I don't reply. Not because I think to be rude.

Because I'm not sure what my answer will be.

Mama Elly must have pestered or browbeat Papa about family mealtime, because she looks smug and triumphant as she asks me to set four places at the trestle table for supper, even though we're rapidly running out of summer.

But when Papa comes in, he doesn't seem the least bit upset at the daylight slipping away. He and Henry are laughing about Sunshine getting her head stuck in a hole, and they settle into their places as I bring the pottage to the table.

"So." I help myself to a wedge of bread, trying to sound carefree. "Fair time will be here soon. Want to hear my ideas about how to get people to come to our booth?"

"Our candles will do that well enough," Papa says over a heaping spoonful of pottage.

The candles I had no part in making. Those candles.

Mama Elly leans across the table to put a hand over mine. "The garden looks beautiful, doesn't it, Osbert? Have you had a chance to look at all of Tick's hard work?"

"My best idea is having some pennants for our booth," I say. "Something fluttery to catch the wind and draw the eye. My apron is all but in rags. I could dye it some pretty color, then cut it up and string the pieces on lengths of cording."

Papa stuffs another bite of pottage into his mouth. I hold my breath while he chews.

I want him to like this idea. To say it's the best thing he's heard in a long while.

"Certainly, if it would please you," he finally says. "As long as you can have them ready by the time Henry and I leave."

"Hurray! I can—wait." I lower my spoon. "What do you mean, *you and Henry*?"

"Tick, dear one." Papa reaches for his ale. "It'll just be Henry and me going to Stourbridge this year."

"No. No." I stiffen. Fists clenched. All but snorting

like a bull. "You're always saying you can't do without my help."

"There's no need for you to go. Henry will be all the help I need."

Henry goes very still. He doesn't even lift his spoon to his mouth. He glances at me with the smallest, sorriest look on his face, and I *know* this isn't his fault, but right now I can't see anything but red.

"You'll be of much more help to me keeping Mama Elly company," Papa is saying, "and once we've gone, cleaning everything in the workshop and the rear yard from top to bottom."

"*Cleaning?*" I am ready to burst everywhere like too-hot tallow. "Henry gets to have all the fun and I have to *clean up after him?*"

"We'll make the best of it, I promise," Mama Elly tells me in her warmest voice. "I've saved back some black currant jam. We can wash our hair with rose-petal water and talk more about growing up."

The very last thing I want to do besides *actually* growing up is talk about it, even if black currant jam is involved. I wouldn't mind my hair smelling like rose petals, but the way she says it makes it one more thing that pushes me out of the workshop, out of the rear yard, and further than ever from my papa.

The way she says it makes me realize how lonely

she's been when Papa and I have been gone to the fair in years past. How long the days must seem when it takes her an age to get from place to place.

"Please." I turn all my pleading on Mama Elly, who can't abide watching small things struggle. "I can't miss the Stourbridge Fair."

She and Papa trade a look. The kind where grown-ups remind each other of what they've already decided.

And my heart plummets, because this means she agreed to go along with something she knew would gut me.

"I'll clean if you want me to." I'm talking fast now, glancing between them faster. "Every last thing in the workshop, whether it needs it or not. But please don't make me miss the fair."

"You've been any number of times. Our booth is cramped as it is with two. There simply isn't room for three." Papa's cheeks are going pink again. "It's one thing when there's a loft with lots of space."

"I'll sleep in the cart! With Trudge!"

Papa ignores me. "Henry needs to know how to set up a booth, how to string the ropes and stretch the horsehide. How to recognize the real ground rent collector and not be swindled by some blackguard."

My father is never going to let me live that down, is he?

I pull in a long, long breath. Let it out slow, like a cat hissing.

"Tick, I know you always have fun at the fair," Papa says, "and I'm sorry you'll have to miss it."

"I don't go just to have fun!" I snap. "I go because you need me!"

I say it like I'd throw a rock—hard, right to the forehead. Sometimes a little bit of hurt gets people's attention.

Now Papa will sit up straighter. He'll lower his spoon and his eyes will go all watery soft and he'll repeat the thing he's always, always said, every time he walked past me stirring tallow or measuring alum.

Couldn't do without you, Tick.

What a help you are.

Only he doesn't.

"I have an apprentice now," he says, as if that explains everything.

The room is still, but for the crackle of the hearth fire. I push my plate away, a slow grind of wood on wood. I haul myself up, step over the bench, and put one foot in front of the other, toward the loft ladder.

All this time I thought I was helping. All those tallow burns. All those sidelong glances from the neighbors, those wrinkled noses and conversations cut short.

All those afternoons I could have spent with Johanna and Lucy, little kids and everything.

I have an apprentice now.

As if nothing I've ever done has mattered to him in the slightest.

⋟ AUGUST ⋞

10

I BARELY SLEEP, and when the sky is that deep purple of almost-light, I slide out of bed and climb down the ladder into the still, empty hall. It's so much cooler down here, and I know I should go right to the kitchen and stir the fire to life, but instead I push open the shutters above my bright table and let in a brick of pale dawn.

In one corner of the table there's a handful of beeswax crumbs. I look closer at Henry's charms and realize they've been stamped inexpertly, that he's had to carve the edges off to make sure the lamb and banner are at the center.

I nearly groan aloud, but the last thing I want is Mama Elly hearing me and feeling like she has to buckle on her brace and come out here to see what the matter is.

All right, that's not true. The last thing I want is Papa catching me sitting here.

I pinch the crumbs into my palm, where I try to form them into a pitiful excuse for a charm.

It looks how I feel. Discarded and in pieces, pushed aside for something newer, something more valuable.

This wax is the closest I'm going to get to making charms like I was promised, so I push the crumbs into my apron pouch. My knuckles brush the gilded brooch with Big Gray as the lion of St Mark.

Knowing it's there makes me smile as I get ready for Mass.

The nave of St Mary's smells like armpit and goat and diaper. Father Leo's voice rises and falls, but I can't get Papa's words out of my head.

I have an apprentice now.

He's always had one, though. He's always, *always* had me, only I don't count.

I knew other candlemakers would never consider me an apprentice, but I thought I counted to my papa.

If I lean to the left and stand on tiptoe, I can see the edge of Johanna's ruffle of curls and the curve of little Waleran's hood where she's holding him.

I could give her an Agnus Dei that Henry's painted, but it won't be the same. She'll take it and be kind about it, but whenever I see her with it, Papa's betrayal will hurt all over again.

The homily today is about St Benedict, how he made up a set of rules for monks to live by but how we would all do well to follow many of them ourselves, particularly the one that says you should always obey without question.

I would not be surprised to learn that Papa slipped Father Leo a pound of candles to speak on this topic today.

"Even when he had to choose between staying with his dying sister and following the rule that monks must sleep nowhere but the monastery, St Benedict thought only of obedience," Father Leo says.

I can't help but perk up, despite my dark mood. There's only one story about St Scholastica, and it's this one.

But Father Leo goes on to talk about other times saints were obedient. Not only does he not call Scholastica by name, he leaves out the best part of the story—the part where St Benedict started packing up to depart her house, to follow the rules because they were the rules and following the rules was always the right thing to do, only St Scholastica had a different idea of what the right thing was.

She knew she was dying, even though she couldn't

bring herself to tell her brother, and she wanted him to stay the night and continue their conversation because it would be the last one they'd have. That was the right thing—to be together while you could, for as long as you could.

But St Benedict refused to listen, so St Scholastica prayed aloud that God would send a storm bad enough that her brother would be forced to stay at her house whether he liked it or not. Right away the rain sheeted down and the winds whipped up, so strong that St Benedict couldn't even open her door.

Then St Benedict got angry at her for making him break the rules. St Scholastica replied, "See here, you weren't going to do the right thing on your own, so I asked God to do the right thing. And He did."

When Father Leo tells everyone to *ite, missa est* at the end of Mass, I don't fling myself outside. I don't flood along with the other kids into the churchyard. I drag myself into the sunshine and perch my rump on the low stone wall near Trudge.

Even *he* gets to go to the fair.

Henry comes around the corner. At first I figure he's here to bring the cart for Mama Elly, but he merely ruffles Trudge's stubby forelock, then sits next to me on the wall.

I have nothing to say to him. September's all but

upon us and he still hasn't asked for my help. Every evening after supper, he insists on painstakingly daubing paint onto charms, then muttering curses as he wipes it away, night after night, while glancing at Papa every other moment.

At length Henry says, "I wish you could come to the Stourbridge Fair. It's not right that you can't."

I glare at him sidelong. "You could have said as much. You could have stood up for me."

"I wanted to." Henry sighs. "I just . . . didn't think it was going to help matters."

I try to keep glaring, but I can't. He's right. It would have only made things worse.

Lucy and Johanna are in the churchyard with their little brothers and sisters. One of them found a hoop, and the older kids are bickering over how to play with it.

I wish Lucy or Johanna would notice I'm sorrowing and come sit with me, or even call me over, but I'm also glad they haven't.

Especially Lucy, who wouldn't hesitate to explain in detail how she'd told me so. Especially Johanna, who would pity me.

They're not here, but Henry is.

"What really hurts is Mama Elly." I run a thumbnail over the stone. "That she agreed with Papa. Forbidding me from going to the fair."

"If it makes you feel better, you were never forbidden," Henry says cheerfully. "You merely weren't invited."

"I just thought she knew how much the fair meant to me."

"Why doesn't she go as well? Why doesn't your whole family go to Stourbridge?"

"Mama Elly . . . doesn't take much comfort in crowds." I pick the least flagrant words like she'd want me to. "There's a lot of walking to be done, too, which is hard for her betimes."

Henry draws a quiet breath, like he hadn't thought of it that way. "So there'll be no talking her into it, then."

I shake my head. "She'd be the one who could convince Papa to change his mind, and she has no intention of doing so."

"Maybe I'll try to persuade him," Henry says. "I'll explain how I've never been to the fair and it'd be a great help if you were there to show me what to do."

"You've never been to the fair?" I can't keep the surprise from my voice. "Oh, you are in for a treat! There's acrobats and trained beasts and so many different kinds of food that you'll want to try them all—especially the spicy things from Saracen lands—and thousands of things to look at and if we're lucky, the fortune hen will be back!"

"The *fortune hen?*"

"Oh yes!" It's hard to stay angry when I'm talking about the fair. "You ask her a question, then you put down two little piles of grain, one for *yes* and one for *no*. Whichever the hen eats from first is your answer."

Henry smirks. "I reckon you buy the grain from the hen's keeper."

"Well. That's true. But the fortune hen is never wrong. Last year, she had a space on Garlic Row just down from ours, and I got to watch dozens of people ask her questions." I grin. "She was right every time!"

"Did you ask her a question?"

I scowl. "I was going to, but then that scoundrel Simon had to ask the hen, *Are you delicious?* When she answered *Yes*, her keeper was furious and packed her up and took her to another row."

Henry laughs till he notices the look about me. Then he pretends he was only coughing.

"If there's one bad thing about the fair, it's Simon," I say in a dark voice. "His papa is a wax chandler, and the fair wardens always put our stalls side by side since we both sell candles, but Simon tells anyone who walks past that our candles are rubbish and belong in the cooking pot with the rest of the animal scraps. One year I hit him in the mouth when he said it, but *I* was the one who was punished."

"Wax candles are costlier than ours, though," Henry says. "Wouldn't it be a good thing for everyone to have the booths close? So people who want something finer can have it, but people without means can have something, too?"

I snort. "Not to hear Simon talk. He's sure everyone would buy the costlier ones if they had no choice."

"See?" Henry smiles. "This is why you must come to the fair. If for no other reason than to show me what's worth seeing and tell me what's worth knowing."

I slump on the wall and stare at my dangling feet because my throat is slowly closing. This will be the first year I won't get to see the fortune hen. No tumblers, no jugglers, no music. No spicy food, no new faces, no new voices.

Not this year, and by the look of things, never again.

"I wish things were different," Henry adds, "but it seems your father is a lot like mine. Once he says something will be so, it'll be so."

"But just because something is so, doesn't make it right."

Henry shrugs. "Mayhap. But it's still so."

"Hey!" Lucy is marching toward us. She's got Waleran on her hip and there are two small barefoot girls trailing behind her, but she glares at Henry like a cat you've just awakened. "Leave Tick alone. Haven't you done enough?"

Henry holds up both hands. "Beg pardon. I—"

"She's *upset*," Johanna adds sternly. "What have you been saying to her?"

"Nothing!" He's alarmed now, jumping off the wall and backing up. "She's sad about not going to the fair and I'm just trying to lift her spirits!"

I go cold all over. I think my mouth is hanging open.

"Why'd you have to say that?" I whisper, because the wound is still too raw for me to even think of telling others.

Especially Lucy, who will lift one eyebrow and ask questions that'll make me squirm.

Especially Johanna, who will want to comfort me, to welcome me into a world where girls don't get to go to the fair, where instead they eat black currant jam and talk about growing up, as if that's good enough for them.

Johanna turns to me. "You're not going to the fair? You *always* go to the fair."

Lucy turns on Henry. "How *dare* you break a confidence? That was clearly not your news to tell."

"I must go," Henry mumbles, and he turns on his heel and flees up the path toward the front portal of the church where the grown-ups are.

Lucy watches him till he's gone. She's likely remembering that afternoon in the goldsmith's shop, how Henry was there when her father humiliated her. How he said nothing while it happened.

"Henry's all right," I finally manage, and I'm a little surprised to realize I mean it. "None of this is his fault. My father's the one behaving as if I've spent the last five years just playing with tallow instead of learning the trade as well as any boy could."

"Your work is beautiful," Johanna assures me. "I can't wait to get my Agnus Dei. I'm going to wear it around my neck every day as soon as Waleran doesn't grab everything he sees."

I study my feet. "Only that's not going to happen, either. Remember how I said that Papa promised making charms would be my job this year? Well, he gave the task to Henry along with all the others."

Instead of bristling with indignance, Lucy and Johanna both nod like they expected nothing more. Like this sort of thing is commonplace in the world I'm so newly arrived in where there are no papas, only *fathers*.

"Henry's trying," I add, fighting to keep the bitterness from my voice, "but his work is not something I'd give a friend, and it'll be a miracle if he finishes a single Agnus Dei before the fair. So I'm sorry. I suppose you'll have an extra braid of onions this year."

Johanna is trying to keep smiling, and I'm upset all over again because I have to break my word to her, and she's sad now, too.

So I reach into my apron pouch and dig out the

handful of wax crumbs from the bright table. The warmth of my body has softened them, and when I curl them into my fist, they cling together like friends in a tight hug. I jab my thumb into the middle like it's the Agnus Dei mold, then offer the wax to Johanna.

"There you are," I say with a kind of lofty, overdone pride that makes her smile. "Not quite an Agnus Dei. More . . . St Scholastica of the Crumbs. Patron saint of slighted daughters."

Lucy peers at the little jut of wax. "Better give me three of those, then. For me and each of my sisters. Slighted daughters all."

"You—want a charm now?" I ask.

"I didn't want an Agnus Dei. Those are for people with somewhere to go." Lucy's voice is way too quiet for her. But then she pushes out her chin and adds, "A pity you're not going to Stourbridge, then. Likely there are plenty of slighted daughters who'd line up three deep to get Scholastica's blessing."

"You'd bring in so much silver that your thumb would get tired and your papa would have to buy you a mold of your own," Johanna says cheerfully.

She says it purely joking, but for the longest moment, I stand there staring.

I could press and paint my own charms. I could sell them at the fair. They'd be ten times as good as Henry's and I'd make a pile of silver and my father would have to admit that he can't do without me.

Papa believes he's doing the right thing by replacing me with Henry just because other people think he ought to. He is like St Benedict, who thought doing as he was told was the right thing to do, but Scholastica understood that sometimes doing the right thing means breaking the rules.

I couldn't do it alone, though.

I glance between my two best friends. At least I hope they're still my friends. We are relearning how to share things when our worlds are so very different from one another's.

Besides, even when we were for-sure friends, it was no small matter to ask Lucy for anything. She has this way of letting you dangle like a spider on a thread, spinning and spinning, while she puts one finger to her chin and takes her sweet time.

But I want us to share things again, and I have to hope that they do, too.

I gesture for Johanna and Lucy to come closer. Trudge can keep a secret, and Waleran is too little to know what one is. I lower my voice and say, "I have an idea. But I need your help."

11

AT FIRST they think I'm joking.

I'll get up very early and bring the brazier and oiled canvas out to the stream where no one will see. I'll paint at night, by candlelight. Once it's fair time, I'll walk the miles to Stourbridge, arrange the charms on a tray around my neck, and sell the lot. The fair is big enough that I can keep my distance from Papa and our booth. All I need is beeswax for the charms and a breadboard for the tray.

When Lucy realizes I'm as serious as the grave, she grins. "Beeswax, I can help you with. Consider it stolen. If *Father* finds it missing, he'll just blame Hodge."

"*Borrowed*," I insist, even though I wouldn't exactly be upset if Hodge got his hide tanned. "Once I sell the charms and pay the lepers their fee, I'll buy your papa a new brick of wax. He'll never know it was gone."

Lucy shrugs. "If you're sure."

Johanna helps Waleran over the low stone wall so he can toddle after Adam. She isn't quite looking at me. It's harder to tell what she's thinking than it is with Lucy. Lucy's every feeling passes over her face like clouds across the heavens.

At length Johanna says, "I want to help, but I'm worried that my papa will notice if one of his breadboards goes missing. Even an old one. He keeps his distance from me enough as it is. I don't want him wroth with me besides."

"It'll just be for a sennight," Lucy points out, and even though she's not using her Lucy voice, the one that cuts like a double-edge blade, Johanna flinches anyway.

"That's all right," I tell Johanna. "I'll think of something else. Perhaps I'll lay a cloth on the ground."

"What do *you* want?" Lucy demands, and I frown at her before I realize she's talking to Henry, who's edging back up the path.

He gestures to Trudge, still resting peaceably in the shade of a yew tree. "I've come for the wagon. Master Osbert says it's time to go."

Lucy nods stiffly like she's giving him leave, then leans close to me and whispers, "Tonight I'll put the wax in a basket near the ford by your house. Where we used to play."

Then she grabs Johanna by the sleeve and they're off, over the stone wall and into the churchyard, where they fall into whatever game the younger kids are playing. Something with a hoop and a stick.

I'll be making my own charms. I'm going to the Stourbridge Fair after all. I'll sell the lot and have a pile of coins to give to Papa. No one will go hungry this winter despite the paltry number of candles and those ham-handed Agnus Dei charms.

Papa will see for certain how he can't do without me.

Henry is quiet as he untethers Trudge. "I'm sorry, Tick. I thought they already knew."

It slides in like a splinter. Sharp and crippling.

So instead of begging his pardon for the way Lucy and Johanna took up for me and chased him off, I simply climb into the wagon and let someone else carry me for a change.

I get up when it's still dark. I wrap the brazier in the oiled canvas along with a loop of cording, and I plunge my arm deep into the barley cask, all the way to the bottom, where Papa hides the Agnus Dei mold. For all my jesting, I'm not fool enough to believe that fair-goers will buy a wax charm made with the imprint of my thumb.

I drop the precious bit of gold into my apron pouch,

then unbank the fire enough to reveal the coals and scoop a few into an old cow horn.

The sky is the deepest purple as I make my way to the stream. It's high summer, but there's still a hard chill to the air and the dew on the grass, and I hurry, pressing the clanking bundle against my middle.

This place has always been a favorite of mine. There's a slope in the bank that makes it easy to come near the cheerful water, whether you need to fill a bucket or wash tallow from your hem or watch dragonflies with your two best friends.

I've just set down my bundle when the brush rustles and I go still.

Henry. He heard me coming down the ladder and—

But it's Lucy who steps out of the undergrowth, followed by Johanna. They're wrapped in cloaks, and Lucy is carrying a basket over her arm.

"Wh-what are you doing here?" I whisper-stammer, and as I scramble to protect my bundle from an onslaught of younger kids, I nearly kick over my horn full of coals.

Lucy holds out the basket and grins. "Helping."

"Don't worry," Johanna adds. "The little ones are still abed. It's just the pair of us."

I take the basket and peek inside. A brick of beeswax peeks out of a tangle of dishrags.

My heart is still racing. I don't know how to tell them I don't want help. I don't *need* help. That one set of bumbling hands is bad enough, and three of us crashing around in the greenwood might raise eyebrows where a single girl might be overlooked.

But just as I clear my throat to say it plain, Johanna reaches beneath her cloak and hands me a warped breadboard.

"Please be careful with it," she whispers.

I hold it against my chest. Johanna wants us to share things again. Lucy, too, considering how much wheedling and promising each of them must have done to have a morning to herself.

Which they've decided to spend with me, doing something that neither of them stands to benefit from, but that's important to their friend.

In a trice I get the brazier set up. Johanna and Lucy gather tinder and wood, and I light the fire with coals tipped gently from the horn. As the sky lightens, we eat some bread ends that Johanna brought and watch the beeswax melt.

"You're really doing this," Johanna whispers, but not in an accusing way. More in wonderment that something so big is possible for someone she herself knows. "Just going to . . . walk to the fair. Without your father's leave. Without him even *knowing*."

I nod. The more I think on it, the surer I become.

"Did you plan any of it?" Lucy asks. "Sounds like you mean to throw a rucksack over your shoulder and skip off to Stourbridge without a care in the world, like you're in some sort of fairy story."

"Yes, I *planned* it," I reply, a little testily, because what else would she call me asking the pair of them for help?

"Won't you get in trouble?" Johanna asks.

"Not if Papa doesn't find out," I reply.

Lucy frowns. "But if you hand your father a pile of silver from selling the wax charms, won't he want to know where it came from?"

I almost say, *I could just give the lot to the lepers.* But one reason I'm doing this at all is to make sure my family has enough to eat this winter, since Henry has slowed the work down.

Then I start to say, *Or I could just put the coins in Papa's purse when he's not looking.* But then he wouldn't know how helpful I am, since he wouldn't know that I'm the one—and not Henry—who made charms beautiful enough that people parted with coin for them.

"Perhaps I won't get in trouble," I reply slowly. "Papa never said I *couldn't* go to the fair, only that I couldn't go with him and Henry."

Johanna's face is pale. Even Lucy looks skeptical.

"All right, yes, it's likely he'll be upset at first," I admit, "but I'll save back an Agnus Dei and show it to him, then pour the money into his hands. Who can possibly stay upset when their hands are full of silver?"

Especially when it's likely that trade will be slow this year, and the number of candles not what Papa was hoping and the quality inconsistent.

"What about Mama Elly?" Johanna asks. "The fair lasts three days, does it not? And then you have to walk to Stourbridge and back? She'll be worried to death should you just vanish for a sennight."

I sit back on my heels. My guts full of worms.

Mama Elly will spend the whole time crying, spun into panic, and there'll be no one here to keep her company. She has a hard time walking long distances, so she won't be able to ask her housewife friends in town if they've seen me. Trudge and the wagon will be gone, so she won't be able to cart herself.

And when she tells Papa how she spent the sennight, he'll never forgive me for causing her such pain.

"I'll think of something," I reply quietly. "I want to go to the fair, but not if it means that Mama Elly suffers."

"You could just tell her," Johanna offers, and I nod, because I don't want to explain.

While the wax melts, Lucy tears my threadbare

apron into long strips and braids them into tight, narrow lengths of rope. She says I can use them to help steady the breadboard by looping them under the bottom, then around my neck. Johanna gives me some green thread to embroider a new apron and explains how they worked the pattern.

When the wax is almost ready, I show them how to cut the loops of cord. We roll out the canvas and arrange the loops.

Now it's time for the fun part—pouring each plum-sized disc of wax and pressing the mold against it. Each charm must be poured and pressed right away, before the wax hardens.

I reach into my apron pouch for the Agnus Dei mold, and along comes the gold brooch with Big Gray with it.

Last year I stamped my first set of charms with Papa's big hand gently guiding my own. All the while he spoke of how hard to press, how to pull the mold straight up so the picture of the lamb and his banner would be clear.

When the lot came out flawless, Papa said the job would be mine next time. He gave me a hug. He told me how proud he was of me, and at the fair, my charms barely lasted a day before every last one left with a happy traveler.

I roll the Agnus Dei mold in my palm. I fight the urge

to heave it into the woods. Only months ago I couldn't wait for this moment. Now I must tiptoe and sneak like some sort of felon.

So much has changed in just one year.

I grit my teeth. I let the Agnus Dei mold fall back into my apron pouch, then I grip the brooch and press it firmly into one of the discs. I know it's meant to be the lion of St Mark, but cast in wax, it looks even more like Big Gray.

I press another, then another. Enough for Lucy and her sisters, and Johanna and hers.

But then I keep going. I make three whole rows of charms with the brooch. Maybe Lucy is right. Perhaps there'll be slighted daughters at the fair who'll want the blessing of Scholastica and a very large, shrewd, discerning cat.

Cats may be the perfect patron for slighted daughters. They're patient when they must be. They survive on what's given them, or what they can take on the sly.

They belong to no one.

After the fourth row using the brooch, I switch to the Agnus Dei mold. Not every traveler will see value in something peculiar, and I must remember why I'm making charms in the first place.

I offer Johanna and Lucy a chance to try the Agnus Dei mold, but both shake their heads. They seem content to watch me press charms, chewing peacefully on bread ends.

It's only once the work is finished and they've bundled themselves in their cloaks and slipped away, back into the never-ending wiping of noses and comforting of tears, that I realize what kind of help they thought to offer.

For someone without a lot of time to herself, being together while you can, for as long as you can, is the most precious thing there is to give.

The Agnus Dei charms take hardly any time to paint. I finish them in three nights, settled happily at my bright table long after everyone has gone to bed, when the only light is the flame of one of Henry's first candles that I sneaked out of the cast-off bucket.

It's not the same, though. I feel like I'm trespassing, like I have no business at this table I've spent so many hours at in years past.

Then it's time to paint the Scholastica charms. I lay one across my palm and consider it. The picture is pressed into the wax instead of standing in relief, and there's less detail to the background. Big Gray's frown of judgment comes through even though it's tiny.

With an Agnus Dei you must paint each one the same way. The lamb must be white. The cross on the banner has to be red, and the grass he's sitting on must be green. If it's not just so, travelers won't buy them. I'm not sure why—they know our wax isn't from Easter candles, so the paint shouldn't matter, either—but it does, so that's how we paint them.

A Scholastica charm is just wax, though. There's nothing holy about them, even if the wax has been blessed, so it doesn't matter how I paint them.

There are many slighted daughters out there, and each one is slighted in her own way.

So I paint each Scholastica charm differently.

Big Gray is brown tabby in one, like Sunshine, and orange in another like the Fox. Sometimes the cat is sitting in a field, other times on a floor of dirt or flagstones. Once against a night sky full of stars.

By the time I'm finished painting, I have four dozen perfect Agnus Dei charms, each the same as the one before, and two dozen Scholastica cats, none the same as the next.

Before I wrap them in scraps of linen to keep them safe—and secret—I hold one of my Agnus Dei charms next to one of Henry's, laid out to dry on the corner of the table. His paintwork is better than it was, but nowhere near the same as mine.

I've had years to learn a steady hand and an eye for mixing color. I know how to paint in layers to keep the colors from being too pale. It's not his fault his charms aren't as good as mine, but if he's not willing to listen and learn, there's not much I can do to help him.

This will be a gooseberries-and-privy moment for certain. For both Henry and Papa.

But it gives me an idea.

⇒ SEPTEMBER ⇐

12

I BLINK AWAKE to a gentle tap on the floorboards. Across the dark loft Henry shifts, then there's the soft rustle of him gathering the rucksack he packed last night. Then the pad of footfalls and the squeak of ladder rope.

Papa and Henry are getting ready to leave for the Stourbridge Fair.

I know, because last year, and the year before, and the one before that, I was the one waking up to that tapping.

I was the one shivering my way out to the byre to feed Trudge and trick him into standing still long enough to be harnessed.

I was the one standing in the cart, carefully packing

bundles of candles in their lineny swaddling like a row of kitten nests.

I was the one leading Trudge straight into the rising sun along the road to Cambridge, elbow to elbow with my papa.

It would be better for my plan if I pretend to sleep through their departure. The less Papa suspects, the better chance I have to succeed.

But the soft murmur of voices is too much for me, and I slide out of bed, put on my cloak against the chill of rising autumn, and climb down the ladder.

Mama Elly is awake, her hair in a night braid down her back, packing up bread and cheese by glowing hearthlight. I slip past her, into the workshop.

Beyond, in the rear yard, there's the creak of cart wheels and Trudge's footfalls in the dirt. Henry must be bringing the cart up to the workshop door, because Papa is fussing over packing that's been done for days.

The candles. The horsehide tent and its carefully bundled ropes. The wood for sawhorses and a trestle to form a counter. Bedrolls, blankets, rucksacks. Hundreds of linen bundles, each containing a pound of candles of different grades and sizes.

There really may be five hundred of them. As many as Papa had hoped.

It's hard to keep my face still. If I hadn't planned to

make my own way to the fair, I'd likely be screaming down this whole yard.

"Tick." Papa sounds surprised to see me. "Good morning, dear one. Come to see us off?"

"Come to make sure you aren't forgetting anything," I tell him. "Your eyes and all that. Especially in the dark. Henry won't know what's missing the way I will."

Papa grunts. "Very well, I suppose that can't hurt. Thank you."

The cart creaks up to the workshop door. Henry loops Trudge's lead around a post, but that won't do for Trudge. I go and hold his halter, reminding him to be a good boy even though both of us know that's unlikely.

"I must say, Tick, I'm proud of the way you're taking this," Papa tells me as Henry loads the wagon. "I thought for sure you'd be sulky and difficult. Eleanor is right. You really are growing up."

"Ah." My face makes a smile because I know I'm supposed to be happy to hear that, but everything inside me feels heavy all at once. "I'm a child, you know."

Papa musses my hair. "Not for long, though."

"Anything else to load into the cart?" Henry appears in the doorway.

As I'm glancing around the workshop, checking to be sure nothing's been overlooked, Papa says, "Seems good to me, son. Let's get our breakfast from the mistress and be off with us."

Good thing it's dark. No one can see me scowl.

Mama Elly tucks a whole rucksack of food over Papa's shoulder and hugs him for a long time. Then she fusses over Henry awhile, worrying that he ought to have a thicker cloak and does he have clean hose?

Henry goes bright pink, even in the dim light, and Papa collars him in a gentle and playful way, leading him out of the kitchen.

"Enough of the mothering, Eleanor," he calls over his shoulder. "You have Tick for that."

I don't know what I like least—that I only get mothering now and not fathering, or that Henry doesn't get any mothering at all, or that it's something to throw around in jest, as if changing how you love someone is funny somehow.

Papa takes his place at Trudge's head and directs Henry to the donkey's other side. They'll take turns leading him. It's a two-day walk to Cambridge at an old beast's pace, but the miles will melt into stories about Papa as a boy, or cute things I did as a baby, or why bird wings and butterfly wings are so different, or whether that silk merchant from Córdoba who speaks ten languages will turn up at the fair again this year.

Mama Elly insists that she and I wave Papa and

Henry down the road, which is harder than I expected it to be, even knowing I won't be far behind them.

Papa always plans on two days to get to the fair, mostly due to Trudge being difficult and unsympathetic to our family's well-being, even though it keeps his own guts happy. I know I can make it in a single day. All there is to do is follow the road.

Ever since Lucy accused me of not having a plan and Johanna asked about Mama Elly, it's occurred to me that they meant have I thought of things beyond making the wax charms.

If I rush off toward the fair today, I'll risk bumping into my father and Henry on the road. Papa and I have traveled that way enough times that the housewives and goodmen at the places we usually stop to rest will recognize me and want to know why I'm not with my father, so making the trip all in one day will keep me from needing a place to stay.

So I must wait until tomorrow to set off.

These hours are the longest of my life.

Mama Elly makes griddle cakes and honey, which are delightful, but then she insists on spending the day washing all the bedclothes and asking me if there are any boys I have an eye for. She laughs when I wrinkle my nose like I smelled something bad.

After supper I finish embroidering my new apron's

waistband with Johanna's green floss, and murmur *uh-huh* in all the right places as Mama Elly dreamily repeats the story of how she met Papa and how it was love at first sight.

I pretend I have a headache and go to bed early.

The next morning I pack in an extra helping of pottage at breakfast, then offer to sweep the hall. While Mama Elly is humming away in the kitchen, I pull my charms out from their hiding place.

Then I stand back, take a deep breath, and murmur a prayer to St Scholastica. She may be the patron saint of Benedictine nuns, but she's also the patron of *just because something is so, doesn't make it right.*

"Mama Elly!" I put a note of urgency into my voice as I step into the kitchen, holding the charms in both hands in their cloth. "Look what Papa forgot!"

She pulls in a sharp breath. "Saints, how did that happen? I thought he had everything!"

"He can't do without these," I tell her. "We need the money these charms bring in."

She nods, clearly upset, and sighs like she can't believe this is happening.

I wait. Patient like Big Gray and Sunshine and the Fox.

Then I say, "I could bring the charms to him. He and Henry are likely not halfway to the fair. I could catch up easily."

Mama Elly peers at me with a heft to her glance, like she's weighing me for truthfulness, but as far as she knows, there's but one set of Agnus Dei charms in this house, and if they're here, they're not packed in the wagon.

Then she nods to the small pot on the table. "I was about to start the black currant jam simmering."

I don't like misleading Mama Elly, but she's wrong, too, just like St Benedict. She could have told Papa that I should be allowed to keep making candles alongside Henry, or that he ought to keep his promise that making charms would be my task, or insisting that I go along to the fair with them.

I've seen Papa do as she bids him enough times to know there's very little he'll deny her.

Mama Elly knows what working at the chandling trade means to me, even if I count to no one but myself. She could have taken my side at any time, and she didn't.

"Also, I thought I'd stop by Johanna's house on my way back here," I go on. "Her mama's due to have the baby any time now and it'll likely be hard going, so Johanna is hoping I can help manage her little brothers and sisters. I want to see if I'm needed yet."

Mama Elly's whole face changes at the mention of a baby, particularly a baby that'll have a rough time being born, and a mama that will struggle, too.

"Oh!" She clasps her hands in front of her heart. "I don't see why not. That's so kind of you, Tick."

"Johanna wants me to sleep over there," I say. "The little ones are really worried about their mama, and Johanna will be on her own with them. Her aunties and the neighbors are sure to have their hands full with the birth and the new baby."

Mama Elly's face crumbles a bit. "I wish I could help. But without Trudge and the cart, there's no way I can—"

"I know," I cut in, talking fast, "and everyone knows how much you love babies, and how much you want to help, but no one expects you to walk all that way. I can, though, and my friend needs me."

"Of course," Mama Elly says, recovering. "A girl should have friends. Of course you must help if you can."

"So if I'm not back right away, you won't worry, right?" I ask, and it takes everything I have to keep my eyes on her and not give all my attention to wrapping up the charms in their linen. "Even if it's a few days?"

Mama Elly shakes her head firmly. "Give my best to Johanna's mama, all right? Off with you. The black currant jam will keep until you're home."

It's everything I can do not to squeal out loud. Instead I pack the charms carefully into a rucksack, along with the breadboard Johanna gave me, and the lengths of braided linen that Lucy made from my old apron.

As I set out on the road toward Cambridge, I wave at Mama Elly over my shoulder, just like Papa did, and I try not to think how she's right back where she always is during fair time. Alone in the house with only herself for company.

She'll have the garden to fuss over. The cats, if they'll let her.

It's a gorgeous day. The sky so blue it hurts my eyes. The sun is warm on my cheeks, but there's the smallest whisper of breeze to keep off the swelter of last month. I swing my rucksack and skip a few measures, laughing aloud. I might not be at Papa's side, but I'm on my way to the Stourbridge Fair.

In fact, it might be fun to be at the fair without Papa. As much as I like selling candles, there's only so much to see from behind our booth's trestle counter. I can never shrug off the feeling that I'm missing out on some wonder as I explain yet again how candles made from suet are costlier because they burn longer. If I can go where I like with my tray of wax charms, I won't miss a thing.

Besides, Papa can be something of a worryguts. He doesn't love the fair the way I do. Truth be told, if he didn't need to make a trip to Stourbridge to ensure our winter stores, he likely wouldn't.

He insists the fair is perfectly safe, that there are levelookers to catch cheats and thieves, and bailiffs and wardens to keep the riffraff moving along, but he doesn't behave as if he believes it.

On I go, following the road, which is not so much a road as it is a track made by the ruts of cart wheels and the hooves of beasts like Trudge. This time of year it's dry, but I still stay on the verge, where the long grass is nicer on my bare feet.

Around midafternoon the road begins to fill with enough people and carts and animals that I smile outright.

We're nearly at Cambridge, which means the fair is all but upon us!

As I get closer, the church spires stab their way into the sky all bristly like Mama Elly's pincushion. The whole town is pretty, like something you'd want pressed into a wax charm. A charm that blesses your home.

It's hard not to be taken in by Cambridge. This will be my fifth year coming to the fair, and making my way through the city is a sheer delight every time.

St Neots is charming, with its priory and church and pretty houses like Lucy's.

But Cambridge is a beehive, people all over the place and streets packed with carts and wheelbarrows and animals, all of them trying to get everywhere and not a one of them succeeding. The buildings soar three and four stories above me, limewashed white or painted cheerful colors. There's a church or priory or friary on every corner, some with spires that soar up and up till you must tilt your head almost off your neck.

Papa always puts his head down and hurries. The crowds discomfit him, and anyone without obvious business puts him in mind of a scoundrel or a beggar. He's sure every person who passes by wants to sneak candles from his load or beg for alms he can't quite afford to give.

He tells me to duck my head as well, that wandering wide-eyed will only mark us as strangers, and strangers are the perfect target for roguery. He pulls me by the sleeve and bids me tug my hood across my face. The quicker we can get through town, the better, he's always saying. We're here for the fair. There's little for us in the city of Cambridge.

But Papa's not here. This time I get to take it all in.

There's a toll to cross the river, but that's easy enough to sort. I slip in and out of the line waiting at the bridge toll gate until I spot a cart whose goods are heaped high. I settle my rump on the tailgate just as the carter is paying his fee, and when he calls *Walk on* to his oxen, he's got a passenger.

The toll man squints at me, but I put all my attention into splitting a grass stem with my thumb as if I'm bored and grouchy and this is the last place I want to be.

Once I'm across, I slide off the back of the cart and do the exact thing Papa has told me dozens of times never to do. I let my eyes drift up and up, following the lines of the buildings, and I gawk as I join the stream of people moving along the road.

Everyone seems happy. Horses have ribbons braided into their manes and tails, and children are waving toys and playing chase. There are hawkers everywhere, bawling the goodness of meat pies and the freshness of fish, and people bunch around them holding up hands clutching coins.

St Neots has a market, but it's nothing like this. Our market is placid and ordinary, lined up along the priory wall in the same order every Thursday. Nothing worth crowding the streets for, because you well know it'll open when the bells ring for Prime and shutter itself at Vespers.

Here in Cambridge, the Jewish quarter is busy too. Papa says Jewish people have their own way of doing things, but apparently everyone likes the Stourbridge Fair, because Jewish papas with big beards are loading wagons, and boys like Henry are stacking crates, and mamas with babies on their hips are packing food into rucksacks.

It makes me wonder where Henry's mother's hostel might be. He said hard by the church of the Holy Trinity, but that doesn't mean much to me, not when Papa's never let me explore.

I suppose I could always ask a scholar. They're everywhere, in and out of doorways, arms loaded with rounds of barley bread, robes caught on stray nails, laughing and shoving and generally making nuisances of themselves despite being old enough to know better. Half-grown versions of the packs of boys that roam St Neots.

If Henry is any measure to go by, when a boy grows up, he doesn't get things taken away like girls do. Instead a boy gets *more* things. More privileges. More trust from grown-ups. More space to roam. More attention paid to his thoughts and opinions.

It makes me wonder if boys get a growing-up talk like the one Mama Elly gave me, but instead of warnings, they get a glimpse into all the good things coming their way if they can just be patient and worthy enough.

I wander through lanes and around corners, petting dogs and smiling at children and looking at everything for sale. The smell of food drifts like a cloud, and my stomach rumbles. I should have brought some bread and cheese, but then Mama Elly would have had questions.

Unless I'd thought to pack it ahead of time and hide it in the byre.

I have no liking for the idea that Lucy might be right. A plan would have helped this venture considerably.

I turn a corner onto a street that smells of tallow. At once the whiff makes me think of Papa, how he's likely already setting up the booth with Henry instead of me. He'll show Henry how to pound the pegs and stretch the ropes, then shuffle the horsehide over the top and tie it down. They'll set up the trestle and lay out candles of different lengths and girths and quality, from farthing lights to sturdy tapers the length of your arm.

Henry's Agnus Dei charms as well. Papa won't know what to make of them not selling, and Henry will have to tell him.

Henry could have asked me for help. He had a lot of chances to do it, and he never did. If he were here right now, I'd tell him as much.

I look up—and there he is. Not a stone's throw from me in front of a tall, narrow building painted a cheerful yellow ocher. He's holding a platter with something tall covered by a linen cloth, and he's deep in a happy conversation with a girl a head taller than him who can be no one but his sister, Margaret.

I freeze, right in the middle of the gutter and its ooze of filth.

I'm not supposed to be here. I'm supposed to be in St Neots, scrubbing everything in the workshop and getting told how splendid growing up is.

I back away a few paces, clutching my rucksack, but it's too late. Henry and I lock eyes. His mouth falls open.

I am in so much trouble.

13

MY HEART is racing. If Papa finds out I disobeyed him before I have a chance to explain, if he finds out I left Mama Elly by herself when I was to keep her company, if he finds out I walked all the way to the fair without anyone's leave with a rucksack full of ill-gotten wax charms to sell, he'll be worse than angry.

He will never look at me the same way again.

Margaret is glancing toward me now, and she turns to Henry and asks him something. Whatever he tells her makes her lift a cheerful hand and wave me over.

I go at a dogtrot. I'm not sure how I'll convince Henry to keep quiet about me being here until I've sold my wax charms. I just know I must.

As I get near, Henry shifts uncomfortably, like his

underclothes are damp. "Tick, this is my sister, Margaret. Meg, this is Tick. Her father is Master Osbert."

He says it as if everything is ordinary and he didn't just catch me out like a red-handed felon.

Margaret dips her chin politely. Even so, she towers over me and Henry, too. For some reason when Henry told me they were barely a year apart in age, I expected him to be the older one. Margaret looks very young-womanly, way more than even Johanna.

"We were just heading in to help Mama with supper." She smiles at the covered platter Henry is holding. Whatever it is smells glorious, like sweet dough and expensive spices.

I'm fidgeting with my rucksack, glancing at Henry, trying to think what to say.

Margaret's whole face falls. "Oh. You've come to fetch him. Your father needs him after all."

"No!" Henry yelps, too quickly. "That is . . . Tick's come to join us for supper. Even though her father has too much to do and must send his regrets. Isn't that right, Tick?"

"Supper?" I'm not sure I heard him properly.

He pleads with his eyes, same as a dog when it sees you eating, because both of us know the real reason Henry doesn't want Papa to share this meal.

But it's late afternoon on the day before the Stourbridge Fair. There are dozens of things to do to make sure the booth is ready for selling, and Henry isn't helping Papa do any of them. Instead he's here, full of reasons why Papa simply *can't* come to supper and hoping to bribe me with meat and cake to keep quiet and agree.

He's here, when I would give anything to be there, with Papa, doing those ordinary things.

I'm hungry enough to chew off my own arm, though, and if whatever Henry is carrying is part of a supper in a hostel, I can hold my tongue a while longer. Besides, Henry is clearly in no position to carry tales to Papa if he's visiting his family on the sly.

Margaret opens the door and leads us down a long corridor. As we emerge into an open space that's more garden than courtyard, I catch a waft of tallow from Henry's cloak. It's too much, and I snare his sleeve and keep him at my elbow while she moves ahead, across the cheerful green space full of turnip tops and onion fronds.

"You said you'd tell Papa about your parents," I hiss.

So much for holding my tongue awhile.

Henry flinches. "I wanted to. I tried. But all I could think was how he'll want to know why I haven't told him before. He'll think I've been dishonest. He'll wonder what else I'll be dishonest about, and it would be so very little trouble to be rid of me now, when he can drop me in my mother's dooryard."

I sigh, but it's hard to stay mad when Henry is in that very dooryard without his master's leave because he misses his mama, and Margaret, too, and he couldn't give up a chance to sit at table with them for just one supper like nothing had changed.

"Do you really think to throw stones at me, though?" Henry asks. "You're not even supposed to be here! Will a visit to the fair be worth the tanning you'll get if your father catches you?"

"I'm not here just to—" I cut myself off. Henry doesn't know about the charms, and he's not going to. "You're the one who said I wasn't forbidden, just not invited."

Henry lifts an eyebrow. "I doubt your father will see it that way."

"I won't tell if you won't."

He grins and holds out a hand, and we clasp wrists just like grown-ups making a trade.

Margaret is waiting for us at the other end of the garden, and we hurry to follow, threading between the beds along tidy paths lined with straw. When we catch up, she leads us into a big wooden kitchen that smells like onions and sage.

There's a woman behind the trestle board, busily chopping parsnips into chunks. Henry steps forward and puts the covered platter down at one end of the board.

When she looks up from her work and sees Henry,

she drops the knife with a clatter and hustles over and hugs him for so long that I feel a little pang and hope Mama Elly is faring well. Henry hugs her back, tight and tighter, not caring who sees him do it.

When she's done hugging Henry, the woman who must be his mama pulls back and considers me in a friendly way. She's stout through the middle like most mamas I know, and she's wearing a battered apron over a gray kirtle.

Henry opens his mouth to introduce me, then hesitates. Even though he's not exactly happy with me right now, he's clearly trying to work out whether I want his mother to know who I am.

But she claps her hands and squeals, "You're Osbert and Alice's daughter! Saints, I haven't seen you since you were just learning to walk and tipped a dish of honey into your hair trying to climb a tablecloth."

I don't remember that, but it sounds like something I'd do.

She tells me to call her Mistress Bea, then says, "You tell that father of yours that I expect him at my table before he leaves for home."

It's the kind of playful scolding that reminds me of Mama Elly. I nod, my face somehow making a smile I don't feel. Mistress Bea thinks I'm here at the fair with Papa, and she has no idea that Papa thinks she and Henry's father are still living happily together in Norwich beneath the same roof.

I will have to be mindful of every last thing that comes out of my mouth.

Mistress Bea gives each of us tasks. Margaret heads to the deyhouse to make butter and slice cheese, and Henry and I are sent to the hall to sweep and set up the trestle tables.

"I want to hear what you've been up to," Mistress Bea says to Henry, "but everything must be laid for supper before the guests arrive. Once they're settled, we'll have time to sit and talk."

"The scholars, you mean?" Henry asks.

"The guests," she repeats. "It's fair time, so people will pay just about any price for somewhere decent to sleep. The going rate is a shilling per night for a bedroll on the hall floor and hot food on the table twice a day, and I still must turn people away for want of space."

Henry gapes. "But you charge the scholars a shilling per *week*."

"It's fair time." Mistress Bea shrugs. "There's not a bed to be had within two miles of Cambridge. There's not an empty byre, shed, stable, henhouse, or patch of floor, either."

I hadn't thought of that. All the years I've been coming to the fair, I've never once thought of where all the people might stay who come from far afield. Papa and I and the other traders, we just sleep in our tents with our goods.

Only that's not something I can do this year.

The hostel's hall is in the front part of the building that faces the street. Henry and I are each armed with a broom, and he starts on one side of the spacious chamber while I start on the other.

I pull the bristles dutifully across the floor, but now I can't think of anything but where I'm going to sleep tonight. It's one thing to promise to sleep in the cart with Trudge, but he'll be in the common pasture with the other animals, and the cart will be securely tied behind the booth where Papa will walk past it all the time to get to the nearby privies.

Across the room Henry is sweeping around the bed-rolls and folded blankets stacked against the wall two and three deep. He could have just told Papa about his family instead of leaving him to set up everything by himself. He could have simply been *honest*.

My broom stops. I grin outright at my dust pile. Henry still owes me a favor, and now I know what that favor will be.

I've never thought to wonder what it's like to stay in a hostel, but now I'll get to find out.

○ ○ ○

The guests start trickling in at sundown. They're families mostly, couples with kids of all ages, with the occasional graybeard. Everyone gathers at the trestle table for the meal Margaret and Mistress Bea have laid out—porridge with bacon, a heap of barley bread and fresh herbed butter, and flagons of ale. Each guest, big and small, gets a slice of the sweet raisin cake that was under the cloth.

Margaret and Henry don't sit down for supper with the guests, so I don't, either, even though watching other people eat is maddening. Instead I sit on the floor by the hearth with my rucksack in my lap, checking each charm to be sure it made the journey safely. It's easier to breathe knowing none are broken and the paint isn't chipped or smeary.

The hall is pleasant. There's a low chatter of friendly, contented voices. Grown-ups discussing the happenings of the day, like Papa and Mama Elly do, and the happy squeals of children playing here and there. The clink of earthenware and the scrape of spoons through food. There's a glow of firelight, too, and the soft tread of feet on boards.

But people continue to arrive. I keep hearing the long creak of the front door as Margaret lets them in, and they clatter down the corridor and take the empty places on the trestle benches that people leave once they've finished eating.

Henry is loading wooden plates and spoons into a wicker carryall with handles, much like the one we keep paints in, and Mistress Bea appears again and again with more porridge, more bread, more ale, more cake.

That pile of bedrolls looks a lot bigger now. Even unrolled, they take up a good amount of the hall floor.

I still must turn people away for want of space.

I tie my rucksack securely onto my back, catch Mistress Bea's sleeve, and offer to help. Within moments I'm behind the kitchen, dunking wooden plates into cold, elbow-deep water in a trough that looks a lot like Trudge's, and scrubbing them with sand to get them clean. I stack them in a carryall, Henry disappears with them and brings dirty ones, and I keep at it until it's full dark and Margaret comes to fetch me because all the guests are finally in and fed and settled for the night.

In the kitchen Mistress Bea has a big spread laid out, and the four of us fall on it hungrily. There's the same porridge she gave to the guests, but this batch has more bacon in it, and there's a stewed chicken that falls off the bone.

My hand trembles on the serving spoon. At home we have meat only on special occasions, and a second helping is whispering my name. But I still have an eye on lodging here, so I have an extra piece of bread and butter instead.

"That'll teach me to come home to visit," Henry teases. "Can't put two feet in this place without being set to work."

Mistress Bea smacks his shoulder in a playful way. "When it's just the scholars, it's nowhere near this busy. The neighbors warned me about fair time, but I had to see it to believe it."

"Fair time is likely a lot more fun if you're actually out on the common with the booths and traders," Margaret says.

"Well, at least we'll have a nice pile of silver by the time it's over," Mistress Bea replies.

"But surely you're going to the fair?" I glance between them, but when they don't immediately agree, I squeal, "You *have* to! It's not to be missed, not at any price."

"See?" Margaret helps herself to my second helping of stewed chicken. "Tick thinks we should go."

Mistress Bea sighs. "Meg, I can't leave the house standing empty. The guests come and go at all hours, and it's not a good idea for you to be at the fair on your own. We're still new enough here that there are dangers we know little of."

Margaret groans softly, like this is not the first time they've had this conversation.

"The fair is perfectly safe," I say as I run my bread

through the last of my chicken drippings. "I've been going every year since I was little. Never had so much as a peep of trouble."

"I'd offer to take Meg around, but I must stay with Master Osbert in the booth," Henry says. "It would be quite dull for her were she with me. But what if she went with Tick?"

I freeze midchew.

"Tick's been to the fair for years now." Henry is warming to the idea and does not heed my urgent looks. "She knows it front to back, and she knows how to handle herself."

"Would you let me come with you, Tick?" Margaret asks in a quiet, hopeful voice. "I wouldn't be a bother. Really."

If Margaret comes with me, she'll know about the charms, and she might tell Henry without knowing she shouldn't. I could explain, but she might not want to keep a secret from her brother.

But if I don't agree, she won't get to go. Margaret will miss out on the fair when I have the power to prevent it, and that makes me the same as Mama Elly.

"Of course you can come with me," I tell her, and when she and Henry both smile in the exact same way, it warms me to the marrow.

"I'm glad that's settled." Mistress Bea reaches across the table to put a hand over Henry's. "Now, tell me everything you've been up to."

He doesn't launch into complaints about how bad tallow smells or how heavy a full mold is. How many times he had to retwist wicks till he got it right. Instead he talks about how welcome he feels in our house, how Mama Elly makes sure he's fed and warm, how Papa is generous and patient and has entrusted him with important tasks right away. How interesting the work is, that candlemaking seems simple until you learn more about craftsmanship and tallow blends and varnishes and wick thicknesses.

He glances at me and adds, "Tick knows all about chandling. It must be hard to go from being an only child to suddenly having something like a brother. But I'm glad she's there to help me. I'm glad we're friends."

I smile, even though the amount of help he's asked for of late has been precisely none.

I smile because I'm glad we're friends, too, even when he doesn't do what I think he ought.

When the raisin cake is long gone and Henry is out of stories, Mistress Bea looks toward the window and shakes her head regretfully. "Looks like curfew will ring soon. Henry, best that you and Tick get back to Stourbridge before the gatemen draw the bars for the night. We don't want Osbert to worry about you two."

Henry cuts his eyes to me. He looks almost frightened.

I give Mistress Bea my most winsome smile. "I was hoping I might stay here. I know being in a hostel is old hand to Henry, but I've never done it before."

"Oh, honey, no. That's not possible. You saw the bedrolls in the hall. Do you think there's a handswidth of room anywhere in this house?" Mistress Bea gives a little laugh, like the happenstance still surprises her. "Even the scholars are charging fairgoers. Apparently, it's sixpence to sleep on their damp, cold floor down in the undercroft. And their space is full as well!"

I grip my rucksack. It never occurred to me that she might say no.

"Another time, Tick. That's a promise." Mistress Bea pushes the bench away and rises. "For now, best go along with Henry back to your father."

I catch Henry's eye and say, "It would be such a *favor* to stay here during the fair."

It takes him a moment. Then he says, "Tick could sleep in my old bed."

"We moved it to the undercroft," Margaret replies. "Mama couldn't let a boy sleep on the cold ground when there was a bed standing empty."

Henry looks like someone punched him in the belly.

He hasn't been gone from here six months and already it's like this isn't his home anymore.

But he recovers and says, "Then she can sleep where my bed used to be. Unless you've let the scholars have that spot as well."

Mistress Bea frowns. "It might be fair time, but I won't have strangers in our private chambers. Not for a mint of shillings."

"Tick's not a stranger. She's a friend of mine." Henry turns to Margaret. "Please? It's only for a few nights."

She pretends to consider. "All right. But only because Tick doesn't smell as bad as you."

Henry puts out his tongue at her, and she does the same to him. "Thanks."

For the first time in a long while, I am not sorry that I smell of road dust and garden earth instead of tallow.

Margaret and Mistress Bea start fussing over a parcel of food for Henry to take to Papa.

As Henry is tying his cloak, he leans close and mutters, "We're even."

"Fair enough." I hesitate, then say, "Something's been bothering me all evening. You told Margaret that Papa couldn't come to supper because he was too busy, but if that were true, why would he let you come instead of making you stay to help?"

Henry grins. "Master Osbert isn't busy. Everything

is already set up and ready for custom on the morrow. What he said was that he was going to the Robin Hood and that I was to keep an eye on the booth and not wait up."

I cackle outright, because I should have guessed. Papa and the other traders gather at that tavern every year and sing questionable ballads and drink ale and hear the news and complain about the wardens and laugh about things it's better that I know nothing of.

I've been told not to wait up, but he always asked a neighbor to watch the booth. Not me, because I'm not a real apprentice, and I never have been.

"If he told you to mind the booth, shouldn't you be doing that?" I ask.

"Nah." Henry shrugs. "There's a night watch, and besides, I gave a farthing to the boy in the space next to ours so he'd keep an eye on our booth along with his."

"A boy?" I go cold all over. "Dark hair that needs a wash? A face you'd like to punch?"

"He had dark hair," Henry replies, "but I didn't particularly want to punch him. He seemed an agreeable sort. All smiles."

"Simon," I whisper, and a shiver goes down my back.

Henry must not hear me, because he waves and disappears up the road toward the Barnwell gate.

When he's gone, I push the door to the hostel closed.

Margaret comes behind me to secure the latch. She's holding a candle in a shallow brass dish, and the dancing wash of firelight should make me feel cozy but instead puts me on edge.

Already Papa has so much to overcome this year. The last thing he needs is Simon and his father making trouble.

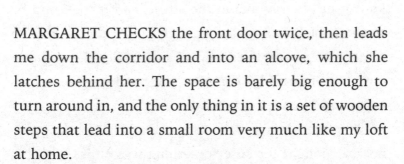

14

MARGARET CHECKS the front door twice, then leads me down the corridor and into an alcove, which she latches behind her. The space is barely big enough to turn around in, and the only thing in it is a set of wooden steps that lead into a small room very much like my loft at home.

It's not as spacious, and there's but one window, but the small size of the chamber makes it snug, like a creature's winter den.

"Here's where Henry used to sleep." Margaret gestures to a patch of bare floor under a sloping eave. "Mama is letting one of the scholars use the bedclothes as well. Some of these poor boys turn up with nothing but the clothes on their backs."

"Kind of like Henry did," I reply with a chuckle, and when her head swivels toward me, I bite my lip hard and wish myself anywhere else.

"What's really going on here?" Margaret asks quietly. "There's something Henry isn't saying, and I need to know what it is."

I hesitate. Margaret didn't have to agree to let me stay here, but Henry ought to be able to tell his own secret in his own time.

So I say, "The reason I want so badly to sleep here is that I'm at the fair without my papa's leave. Henry didn't know until he saw me in the street, and it took him by surprise. He's being kind enough not to tell on me, so please don't carry tales to your mama. She'd march me onto the Stourbridge common and hand me over to my papa, and I'm not ready for that yet."

Margaret lets out a long breath. "Thank goodness. I thought for sure something was amiss with his apprenticeship. That he's not suited to the work, or he's unhappy, or . . . something else."

"No, nothing like that." I think of the candles tucked into the cart, Henry's proud smile.

Margaret tugs a blanket off her bed and hands it to me. She seems easier now that she knows that her brother is in no danger of being sent away. "What are you doing at the fair, then? Why risk your father's temper?"

In the faint light you can really tell that Henry and Margaret are brother and sister. They have the same eyes and round chin, the same thick doe-tawny hair. They look very little like Mistress Bea, who has a slender dark braid and eyes the color of ice in January.

They must take after their father. Papa's friend from another time.

I kneel, open my rucksack, and unwrap one of the small parcels within. It's a Scholastica charm, and I hold it out for Margaret to see. She hasn't yet blown out the candle, and she brings the light closer to examine the circle of wax.

"I made these. Dozens of them." If she's coming to the fair with me, she may as well know the truth. "Some look like this. Some are Agnus Deis. I plan to sell every one and fill my father's palms with silver."

"Agni Dei."

I'm so caught up in my confession that the odd word stops me cold. "What?"

"It's how you say there's more than one Lamb of God," Margaret replies. "In Latin."

"You know *Latin*?"

"Peter is teaching me." Her cheeks are growing pink. "He's one of the scholars in the undercroft. Every day at breakfast, he gives me a new noun to conjugate. At supper, I get a verb that needs declining."

"Oh," I breathe, and then I don't know what to say. Margaret must be even more young-womanly than I thought.

It doesn't seem to bother her, though. She doesn't seem to be losing nearly as much as someone like me.

At length I ask the questions that Mama Elly might, the ones Margaret likely wants to hear. "Are you sweethearts? Do you plan to meet him at the fair? Do you think you'll marry him?"

"*Marry* him?" She laughs. "Goodness no! Saints, I can see it now—a scholar's wife, sweeping the undercroft all day, forgetting what the sun looks like, then putting his supper in front of him and sitting in silence while he reads."

I frown. "Isn't that what you do now? You and your mama?"

"Not at all." She shakes her head so hard her curls bounce. "Wives aren't paid a shilling a week."

Mama Elly is always on her feet, making sure we're fed and warm and our clothing is tidy. She works just as hard as Papa, and if she didn't, there'd be nothing to eat and no fire to cook it on and our house would be cold and dark.

"Peter's nice to look at, is all," Margaret goes on, "and he's funny and kind, and I like learning Latin."

That was part of Mama Elly's growing-up talk as

well, how you'd know a good boy when he cared what you thought and made you laugh and you looked forward to seeing him. Just because a boy showed an interest in you didn't mean you had to be his sweetheart. It was just as important for *you* to like *him*.

I want to ask Margaret what her papa thinks about all this. I want to ask how her papa feels about *her*, being all young-womanly like she is.

Her papa's far away, though, and given how neither Lucy nor Johanna wanted to speak of it, I can't ask this girl I just met about something so sore and bruisy.

Or perhaps it doesn't matter. It must be easier for Margaret's papa, loving a daughter at a far distance and not having to worry about people *getting the wrong idea* if he hugs her in the street.

I place the Scholastica cat on Margaret's palm and gently curl her fingers over it. "You should keep this one. Slighted daughters ought to pull together."

"Slighted daughters?"

"Henry told me about your parents. I hope that wasn't out of turn."

"No, of course not. It's not a secret." Margaret frowns faintly, like she's thinking something over. "But I'm not slighted. Not even a little. If anything, I could use a little less fussing and a lot more time to myself."

I cough a laugh. Margaret is even more young-womanly

than I am, yet she doesn't seem to know that those are other things you lose growing up.

"Your work is beautiful," she says, touching the edge of the disc, "but why must you sell wax charms at all? And why must you sneak around behind your father's back?"

Henry in the rear yard, slowly cutting fat, slowly getting better at it. The cats twining round him, purring, as if one two-legged creature was the same as another.

Johanna's papa holding her at arm's length when he once hugged her tight, right in the middle of the high street.

The quiet of these last few months, how Papa found other places to be whenever I was near. How we never once talked about why fleece was curly and why the sky was blue and not green.

"I must be needed," I whisper. "I must be needed or all is lost."

"But why?" Margaret sounds genuinely bewildered. "Surely your papa loves you for your own sake."

My throat grows tight and hurty. "When someone can't do without you, they'll keep you close for always. That's the same as love."

"I can't agree." She smiles sadly. "When someone needs you, it's easy for them to forget that you're a person who needs things, too. You're always doing for others, never yourself. I think it's better for someone to *want* you around."

"But if someone has no need of you, it's easy to replace you." My voice catches. "Then you're stuck with growing up and becoming young-womanly and caring about boys and babies, when you'd rather be cutting fat and minding the tallow and cleaning molds and all right, yes, smelling to high Heaven, but at least you're doing it *together*."

Margaret is quiet. Her face says she's remembering what Henry said at supper. *Tick knows all about chandling.*

"I know it's not Henry's fault," I whisper. "It's my father's."

"Maybe it's no one's fault," she replies in a gentle voice. "It might just be the seasons turning."

"Well, I don't *want* them to turn!"

She touches a gentle finger to the Scholastica cat in her hand. "When my mother and father decided to live apart, I thought I'd never forgive either one of them. Then there was noise about us moving here, and I couldn't believe they'd force Henry and me to leave the only home we'd ever known."

The cat on the charm is painted gray. The candlelight gleams off the varnish and makes his coat seem real enough to pet.

"I miss my father," Margaret goes on, "but just because

we're not beneath the same roof doesn't mean he cares any less about me, or Henry."

"Or he was happy to be rid of the lot of you," I suggest, and it's so mean that I cringe even as I'm saying it, but she just shrugs.

"Oh, I thought that for some time. There are days I still think it." She meets my eyes steady on. "But he's still doing for us, even at a distance. He convinced my uncle to let Mama run this place as a hostel. He found Henry an apprenticeship so he could make his way in the world. My father always said there's no man he trusts more than Master Osbert to help Henry find a place in trade."

"What about you, though?" I ask. "I bet your father told you to hurry up and become young-womanly so you could be married."

Margaret smiles. "Truth be told, he said the opposite. That I was growing up too fast, and he ought to tie a brick to my head to keep me little forever."

"That sounds like something my stepmother would say," I reply. "Also, do you think it would work?"

She laughs, but it's well enough for her. Being young-womanly is working out fine where she stands.

"I can ask my father if there's a place for you in the tannery," Margaret teases. "He and your father were going to trade sons, did you know?"

"It's not too late to trade daughters," I tease back.

"You could go to St Neots and talk about boys with Mama Elly and watch Henry make candles, and I could stay here and eat raisin cake and learn Latin from the scholars."

Margaret puts out her tongue. "What if I call your bluff? My father's visiting for the fair, so we can ask him if you'd make a good tanner."

I blink. All good cheer gone. "Your papa is coming *here*?"

She nods happily. "I'm not sure which day, but he'll be here before the fair closes. Ooooh, you know what? Don't tell Henry. Let's have it be a surprise!"

"A surprise," I echo in a strained voice, but it's enough to please her, because she bids me good night and blows out the candle and settles beneath her bed-clothes.

In the dark I curl in my borrowed blanket and make my cloak into a pillow. Even if I wasn't sleeping on the floor, I'd still be squirming.

Papa can't know I'm here till I'm ready to hand him silver, but I can't just leave Henry to be blindsided by his father turning up in Cambridge. After visiting his family, he's sure to stop to see his old friend who has a booth in Garlic Row, and if Papa finds out about Henry's parents before Henry himself can tell him, it won't go well for anyone.

I'll find Henry right away tomorrow and tell him before I get on with selling my wax charms.

It's what a friend would do.

When I blink awake the next morning, the first thing I do is rub my sore shoulders.

Then I squeal out loud. The Stourbridge Fair begins today!

If this were any other year, I'd be bouncing out of my bedroll and following Papa up the row to one of the cookshops to get some hot porridge and cider. It would still be dark, and we'd be glad of our cloaks. We'd blow on our hands, and between bites, we'd talk about what we hoped the day would hold.

Instead I sit myself up in Margaret's small chamber. I'm alone, so she must be awake already, helping her mama get breakfast together for the guests.

I pull out Johanna's breadboard and the strips of my old apron that Lucy braided into narrow lengths of rope. I wind them good and tight around each corner of the board, leaving enough to run around my neck. The breadboard feels sturdy when I hold it, the apron rope will help me balance the board, and the orange of the linen will draw the eye nicely.

I pack it all away again, then sit quietly on the floor for a long moment. I'll soon be at the fair, sure enough, but it won't be the same. It will never be the same again.

In the hall the trestle benches are already packed with guests, and the board is groaning beneath a steaming breakfast of porridge and stewed apple compote and fresh rye bread sliced thick. Older children sit on the floor with their food while the smallest ones sit on their parents' laps, poking crusts into their mouths. The big hearth glows bright and lively, which takes the edge off a morning that's already squinting toward autumn.

Margaret bustles among the guests, pouring small ale and taking empty plates and passing the butter. A curly-headed child drops a crust into his mug of milk and tries to fish it out and squalls when his mama scolds him for making a mess. Margaret is at their side in a moment with a wet rag and a kind word.

My stomach drops, and I regret agreeing that she could come to the fair with me. There's no way she's going to leave her mama to do all the work herself, and no way Mistress Bea will let her.

When she reaches for a pitcher on a sideboard, the light gleams off the Scholastica cat around her neck, the cord loop threaded through a length of red ribbon.

Sometimes being a good friend is very difficult.

Sighing, I start loading dirty plates into the carryall.

I hurry back and forth through the garden that spans between the hall and the trough behind the kitchen, bringing clean plates, fetching dirty ones. The sky gets lighter and the sun turns the world gold.

I'm going to miss the opening of the fair. The music. The processions. The proclamation.

All right, I could do without hearing the proclamation. The proctor of the leper hospital has a whiny voice that honks out of his nose like a goose with a bellyache, and I already know not to break the king's peace and to abide by the judgments of the fair wardens. I already know there'll be fines for anyone who uses false measures or tries to cheat the lepers of their fee by selling without permission.

At least most of the fairgoers at the hostel eat quickly. They want to join the procession out of Cambridge toward the fairgrounds, behind the mayor and bailiffs and burgesses.

As the last few trail out, I survey the mess and sigh. There's the trestle board to be washed down and scrubbed. The hall floor to be swept and swabbed. The endless pile of plates and serving platters and spoons to be washed.

"I know it looks like a lot," Mistress Bea says, "but if we're quick at it, you girls could be on your way by midmorning."

Margaret heads to the well for fresh water while Mistress Bea and I set to sweeping the hall floor. The bedrolls are stacked against the wall once more, but there's a strewing of crumbs and dirt and leaves everywhere, and sticky patches of spilled ale that grab at the broomstraws.

"Thank you for letting me stay here," I say. "I've never met a woman set up in trade on her own before."

"I'm not on my own," Mistress Bea replies. "Margaret's here. But I see what you mean. The house may not be mine, but she and I are the ones who put in the work."

Margaret is like an apprentice, and she counts to her mother.

Mistress Bea chuckles and adds, "I like taking care of people, is all, and these scholars are hardly more than boys. They still need some mothering, even if they'd never admit it."

"And mothers don't get a shilling a week," I say, but then I flinch, and not just because I may have gotten Margaret in trouble.

Mistress Bea merely smiles like I just happened across a secret. "They don't, do they? Nor do wives. And we all do the same work."

I think about Lucy and Johanna, how they're always bandaging skinned knees and wiping noses and cleaning up spills.

I think about Mama Elly and her growing-up talks. How it seems like there are rules to it, and one of them is that I must grow up and I must get married, as if the two are intertwined like climbing ivy.

But here is Mistress Bea. She has done her growing up, and she has found a way to keep herself without being a wife.

I wonder if she prayed it into being, like St Scholastica prayed for that storm.

15

IT'S NIGH on midday by the time the hostel is put to enough order that Mistress Bea lets us go. Then Margaret wants to put on a clean kirtle and rebraid her hair and take off her Scholastica cat for safekeeping.

I wait out front because it's everything I can do to keep a smile on my face as I fidget like my underclothes are full of fleas.

Once she's ready, we're off toward the Barnwell gate, calling promises over our shoulders to return by sundown.

Cambridge doesn't have city walls, only the river on one side and a ditch on the other. The ditch is as deep as a fairly tall man and as wide as two horses nose to tail, and it's filled with the chuckings of people's privy buckets.

Given that it's fair time, there's more chuckings than usual.

The day is clear and blue and glorious. We cross the ditch over a sturdy bridge and join the trickle of people heading out the Barnwell road toward Stourbridge. It's not far, perhaps two miles, and Margaret is full of questions about what we should see first and whether she should have left her cloak at home because it's already warm for September.

Her obvious joy thaws me a little. She reminds me of me the first year I came to the fair, how I wanted to see everything and meet everyone. How I cried a little on the last day when the tents and booths started coming down, and how I squealed when Papa told me not to be upset because it would all come back the next year—and so would I.

As we approach the Stourbridge common, the crowds grow thicker and the smells of roasting meat grow stronger. In the fields before Garlic Row are hundreds of tents, carts, and traders settling themselves in front of their goods.

A few stray notes of music plink up, then a lute leaps into a cheerful carol. Right away an organistrum joins it, and some shakers and someone playing the rattlebones. It's coming from a distance, down where Garlic Row meets the road to Newmarket.

I grin and hug myself. There is so much to love about the fair.

"Since you're being kind enough to let me follow after, you should decide what we do first," Margaret says, even as her gaze is pulled toward the bright swirl of woolens and silks and linens in the drapery booths at the far end of Garlic Row.

"Well, the first thing for me is to buy an armband," I tell her. "Everyone who sells at the fair must pay a fee to the lepers. It's how they keep themselves."

Margaret scrunches up her face. "Certainly not from the lepers in person."

"No, from the monks who look after the hospital." I squint and peer ahead. "Look, there's one now."

Only I stop. There are several people gathered near the monk, waiting their turn to pay their fees, but that's not the problem.

I know him. He's Brother Roger. His nose looks like a turnip and he has the kind of red cheeks that Papa says means too much ale. And there's Brother Francis. These monks are here every year, and they know me.

More to the point, they know Papa.

So many people here at Stourbridge are going to recognize me. It won't be long before they have reason to pass our stall to bid Papa good morning and they won't see me there. They'll see Henry instead, and they'll ask questions.

For the first time since St Neots disappeared over my shoulder, I feel a twinge of worry.

It takes a while before we find a monk I don't know. He's a graybeard, and stout, and the sun has reddened the tonsure in his hair so badly it's peeling little flakes into the white curls above his ears. He's holding a fistful of red cloth strips in one hand and a round leather purse in the other. He looks like he'd rather be anywhere but here, and considering he helps run a leper hospital, that's saying something.

"Good morning," I say politely, and I curtsy. "I'd like to pay my fee, please."

"Tell your father to come himself," the monk says to the top of my head.

"It's not for my father." I smile because it feels good to say. "It's for me."

The monk squints at me. "This is new. Women who are up to no good don't usually have such charity toward lepers."

"I'm not a woman up to no good," I tell him, and I hold up my rucksack. "I'm a child, and I have things to sell."

He grunts. "I suppose your coin spends the same as anyone else's. You don't have a cart, so you must be a strolling peddler?"

I nod. Plenty of people come to the fair with goods

on their backs and need only a bit of ground to lay them out on, or else they wander around calling their wares.

"Twopenny, then." The monk holds out a meaty hand.

Something hot turns over in my belly. Papa always handles the fee for our booth. He counts pennies and farthings into a monk's hand while I do the important work of laying out the candles just so.

This is another thing that could have used some planning.

"Well. Ah. Can you take a trade?" I fumble my rucksack to the ground and fish out a charm at random. It unfolds from its wrappings as an Agnus Dei, and I push it into the monk's big hand.

He frowns, then lifts it closer to his face. "Lepers can't eat wax, nor can they buy bread with it. Pennies, two of them, or let someone else forward."

I wring the neck of my rucksack. "But how can I have coins to pay if I don't have an armband that gives me leave to sell?"

The monk turns the Agnus Dei over in his hand, then sighs. "Very well, child. Here's what we will do. You may take the armband, and when you sell enough, come back and I will redeem your charm for threepence."

"A moment ago, you told her an armband cost twopence," Margaret says skeptically.

"Twopence for the armband," the monk replies. "A penny for my trouble."

Margaret frowns. "That's—"

"Very kind of you," I cut in, and I snatch the red cloth from his outstretched hand and pull Margaret away before he changes his mind.

When we're a handful of paces distant, I step behind a tent to secure the armband. Margaret follows, sighing.

"You don't have much of a head for trade, do you?" she asks.

"I have a head for making things work," I tell her, but I smile to show it's all right that she would have done it differently.

I'm glad I practiced putting together my makeshift tray in Margaret's room this morning, because it takes me no time at all to get the linen ropes secured beneath the corners of the breadboard and around my neck. I balance the edge of the tray against my middle and Margaret helps me arrange the charms in two rows, Agni Dei on top and Scholastica cats on the bottom.

"Best to use some of these wrappings to make a nest for them," she says. "That way they won't slide off easily as you walk."

I hadn't realized how different it might be to sell somewhere that isn't behind a counter. In the middle of a crowd, anything could happen. Someone could snatch charms right off my tray, or bump my arm and send them all to the ground.

"Also, best put only a few charms out at a time." Margaret is tucking several wax discs back into my rucksack. "If it looks like something is scarce, folks will want it right away, and they'll pay the price you ask."

Margaret is a lot like Lucy. She's a lot like Johanna, too. In a way she's the best parts of both of them.

Once the charms are settled, I nod to Margaret and we weave slowly through the crowd. It's so strange to be on this side of the counter, almost like a fairgoer myself.

That thought makes me smile.

Even though I usually begin with the animals, I turn us toward the drapery row where traders have ell upon ell of cloth laid out for sale. While Margaret squeals over the colors and patterns, I show my tray to anyone who'll look at it.

Margaret is wistfully rubbing her thumb along a sample of linen. Next to her at the trestle counter is a woman in a veil so tight it cuts a line in her forehead, and lingering an arm's length distant is a girl about my age who looks like she was born scowling.

"Can I go now, Mother?" the girl groans. "I don't *care* about tablecloths."

"I care little for what you care about." Her mother keeps flipping through cloth samples without looking at her. "We didn't come here for you to run wild."

The girl sighs mightily and folds her arms tight, like a shield.

Betimes people feel sorry for me because my mama died when I was too small to remember her, but just because your mama bore you doesn't mean she won't slight you if she has a mind to.

I approach the girl, smile, and hold out my tray. "Do you care about wax charms? I made these myself, with my own hand."

The girl sighs again, deep and gusty like Trudge when he is tired of pulling, and pretends to look at them.

Then she stops and really looks at them. She whispers a finger over the Scholastica cats painted gray and striped and orange. "You made them?"

I think about how Lucy said there'd likely be lots of slighted daughters at Stourbridge, girls who want to wander the fair instead of endlessly looking at tablecloth linen.

Girls who'd line up three deep just for the chance to be seen.

"I've never seen one like that," the girl goes on. "What'll they do?"

An Agnus Dei will protect you while you're traveling. A St Sebastian medal keeps illness away. A sprinkle of holy water helps along just about anything.

But a Scholastica cat is just wax.

"They . . ." I think of my friends on the stream bank, early, cold and damp, all of us together just like we once were. "They give you the blessing of Scholastica."

The girl frowns, but not in a mean way. More like she's not sure whether to believe me.

"It's true! I want good things for everyone who buys a charm from me." In a lower voice I add, "Especially slighted daughters."

The girl's mother notices me and scowls. "Shoo! Be gone! We'll not be wasting coin on nonsense."

When I don't move fast enough, she shoos me with two bold hands to my shoulder blades, and I go stumbling. Margaret gives her a dark look and we stride purposefully toward the next booth.

Once Margaret's touched every corner of cloth, we wander down by the dairy booths, where housewives and servants line up with their pails and dairymaids hand over kerchiefs full of cheese to delighted buyers.

A man with long red hair buys an Agnus Dei for twopence and promptly hands it over to his wife, who squeals and hugs him.

My first sale! Soon enough my apron pouch will be heavy with coins.

Margaret's eyes are huge as we weave between fairgoers, me holding my breadboard tray over a child's bouncing head and tipping it to miss an elbow. We're close to the river now, and by habit I drift downward, away from it and the clatter of oyster shells underfoot and the drifty creaking of barges on the water. Away from the lightermen with their muddy fingernails and river smell.

Near the horse market, I sell one Agnus Dei after another to travelers about to leave the fair on horses they just bought. At the final reckoning, I'm four lambs lighter.

True to her word, Margaret hasn't been a bother. She's followed where I've led, but now she turns to me, grinning big. "Let's go see Henry! I want to see his workmanship. Mama gave me a few coins to spend; mayhap I'll buy some of the candles that he made."

As the words come out of her mouth, I remember how I was going to go right to Henry and tell him about his father coming to Cambridge, hopefully with enough time that he could tell Papa about his family and not get caught flat-footed.

Then I wonder how I meant to do that when Henry must man the booth with Papa, both of them together so Henry can learn how to speak with customers and show off his wares.

Margaret clearly misunderstands my gape-mouth silence, because she rushes on, "That's right, your father can't know you're here. But could you point out the booth? I'll go by myself."

"Ah. Well." I silently beg Henry's pardon. "There's something else."

As I explain, Margaret groans low and slow. "My brother needs to learn to speak up. Not just for himself—for others, too."

I think of all the times Henry *wanted* to say something when ill befell me, yet chose not to because it was easier for him.

"I'll pull Henry aside and tell him our father's coming to Cambridge." Margaret sounds disappointed to be robbed of the chance to surprise him. "If he doesn't find a way to tell your papa about our family, that's his whirlwind to reap. Now show me the booth."

Margaret and I leave the horse fair, cross Garlic Row near the ferry, and move through the tents and hawkers on the townward side. It's midday, and the crowds are thick and sweaty. People walk past with mutton skewers and giant wedges of pease bread slathered in honey and butter and stewed fruit.

My mouth is watering, but I put a hand against my jingling apron and remind myself why I'm here. There'll be plenty of supper at Mistress Bea's table, and I will just have to wait to fill my belly.

Our booth is midway down Garlic Row on the eastern

side. I clutch my breadboard tray with both hands as I lead Margaret toward the row from the townward side, and we crouch behind a tent selling shoes.

Sure enough, there's our booth, right across the row where it always is. The horsehide tent is stretched tight and the trestle board spans the entrance, and behind it stands Henry at one end and Papa at the other. Even at the distance I can tell they're both scrubbed and smiling at fairgoers who pause to look over the candles.

"There," I say, and my heart folds a little at how natural Henry looks behind the trestle counter, how Papa claps him on the back.

How little my father misses me. How little he needs me.

In the booth next to ours, Simon's father stands behind his own trestle board. He's big like a bear, and he likes to draw attention to his fancy tunic by resting both hands on his giant barrel belly. Their tent is made of canvas dyed bright yellow instead of smelly old horse-hide, and—my teeth grind—smart-looking blue and red pennants flutter from poles at either corner.

Margaret waits until Papa is absorbed in showing a housewife some candles, then she straightens her veil and steps into the road, weaving through the crowd like she's been going to the fair for years.

She's halfway across when Simon steps into her path.

He bows, which must seem polite to anyone who's never met him, but Margaret doesn't know enough to put her nose in the air and keep walking. Instead she pauses, smiles, and says something that makes him glance around like someone owes him ten shillings.

I grip the breadboard. I want to dart between them and send Simon flying like I might a flock of crows menacing the garden.

I can't, though. If Simon knows I'm here, it's only a matter of time before Papa does too. Simon would make trouble for me just for the sport of it.

It turns my stomach a little, watching Margaret talk with Simon as if he's any sort of decent person, but it's more than a little satisfying to see him pinken and stammer like someone with porridge for brains.

It almost makes me wish I'd listened a little more closely to the growing-up talk, if there might have been something useful in it.

Their conversation ends with Margaret smiling winningly and saying something that makes the most simpering, fawning look come over him. Then she continues toward Henry behind the counter in the booth.

Simon is left in the middle of the row. The crowd moves around him like a stream past a stone. I cackle aloud at how much of a pudding he looks.

Something tugs at my sleeve and I nearly jump out of

my skin, but it's the girl from the drapery row. The one who thought so little of tablecloths.

"How much?" she asks, gesturing at the charms.

I almost offer her one for nothing. This girl isn't slighted like Lucy or Johanna, but it can't feel good to have your own mama tell you she doesn't care how you feel.

"I'll give you six farthings for that one." The girl points to the cat who looks like Sunshine.

I pretend to think it over, but inside I'm squealing. Papa always sells charms for a penny apiece. He doesn't like to bargain for them since they're not made from proper Easter candles, just wax that Father Leo murmurs an Ave over.

But since there are four farthings in a penny, I'll be coming out ahead if I take the girl's offer.

"All right," I say, and for the first time since I laid eyes on her, she smiles. She drops the coin fragments into my palm and I lay the charm in hers.

Once the girl departs, I fidget with my tray. The longer I stay here, the better the chance someone recognizes me, and if Margaret doesn't hurry up, Papa's going to notice Henry's absence and ask questions.

But Papa has a new customer—a boy, not much older than me, bony like a starving cow and wearing a cloak made of what seems to be dirty washrags. His hair is

cropped close and his neck has likely never had a scrubbing, but Papa is wrapping up a parcel of candles for him.

A big one.

Perhaps the boy is a scholar who prefers to spend
his coin on books and candles to read them by instead
of a decent tunic and a cake of soap. Whoever he is, he
just bought a good number of candles, which makes me
smile in spite of the fact that I had no hand in making
them.

The boy takes his parcel of candles from Papa just as
Henry steps back into the booth and behind the counter.
There's something odd about the boy, the way he walks
head-down and furtive like a weasel with the candles
pressed against his belly. Not like a scholar swaggering
like he owns the whole row.

Like a thief.

But Papa doesn't look upset. He's counting coins in
his palm, so the boy clearly paid.

The boy is three booths down, all but lost in the
crowd. Then he stops in front of a dark-haired youth in
a tunic red as blood.

Simon.

16

"WELL, IT'S DONE."

Margaret appears at my side, and I glance at her just long enough to lose both Simon and the bony boy in the crowd.

"My brother gave all kinds of excuses," she goes on, "but he finally promised to tell your father about our family."

I crane my neck once more, twice, then give up.

Just because Simon is a turd doesn't mean he's doing anything wrong, or the boy, either. Papa would be raising hue and cry right now if something was wrong with the coins, or if he found a candle or two missing from the counter.

"Apparently, it's a great time for a confession, since

your father's in a particularly good humor." Margaret grins. "More than half of their candles have sold already, and it's only the first day of the fair!"

That gets my attention. "You're sure? That can't be right."

Margaret nods happily. "I suppose when people buy their candles in dozens of pounds, you'll sell through quicker than you think."

I peer at our booth, trying to make sense of it. Papa offers a special price to anyone who buys more than two dozen pounds of candles at a time, and a very special price for six dozens or more, but in all the years I've been to the fair, I can count on the fingers of both hands the number of times he's had occasion to give either price.

Even as I'm wondering, another boy comes to the trestle board. He looks a good deal like the first, like someone Mama Elly would put bowl after bowl of porridge in front of, and he doesn't linger or consider. He points to what he wants and holds up six fingers. Before long, he's walking away with the bulging rucksack, when he doesn't look like he's had a good meal in at least a sennight.

It doesn't make sense.

I look down at my tray. At the line of Scholastica cats. Then I turn away from our booth. From Papa's booth.

Father's booth.

I have goods of my own to tend to.

Margaret and I wander through all the rows—timber, iron, wool, leather, even the row where scholars crowd around shelves of books. We're near the skip row, where weavers have all kinds of baskets and mats for sale, when Henry steps into the thoroughfare. His cheeks are scarlet and he's glancing around like he misplaced a gold ring.

Margaret lifts a hand and waves before I can pull her behind the nearest tent. She has no idea that Henry knows nothing about the charms, and now it's too late, because he comes flying toward us like a dog on quarry.

"Did you tell Master Osbert?" she asks in an older-sister voice that would be the envy of both Lucy and Johanna, but Henry barely looks at her. Instead his frantic eyes run over the tray I'm carrying, newly stocked with wax charms.

Then he shoves both hands through his hair and chokes, "Oh God help us."

Margaret folds her arms. "If you didn't tell him, then—"

"It's not that." Henry glances over his shoulder, then narrows his eyes at me. "Tick, where did those charms come from? What are you *doing*?"

I open my mouth to tell him that it's none of his business, but Henry and I are friends. He already agreed not to tell Papa I'm here. He's been sorry all along about what his being Papa's apprentice means for me.

I could tell him about the charms and he might understand, just like I could have told Lucy and Johanna why it was so hard to play with them and avoided all those years of bad feelings.

Henry of all people knows what it is to want your father to think the best of you.

So I say, "I made them. I'm selling them. That's why I came to the fair, because—"

"The levelookers are at our booth right now," Henry cuts in. "Someone's claiming that your father is trying to cheat the lepers *and* gain an unfair advantage."

"He wouldn't!"

Henry nods at my breadboard tray. His eyes are flinty. "The levelookers say Osbert Greenwell is sending his daughter out as a strolling peddler with fine charms at a high price while selling poorer ones in the booth for less."

The fair wardens have all kinds of rules to keep traders from taking advantage of customers—and one another. You can't buy up all of something and then sell it at the same market for a higher price. You must use the king's measures and not ones you make yourself.

You can't sell the same goods in more than one place.

"Papa doesn't even *know* about these!" I grip my tray tighter.

"Which is why right now he's swearing on every

saint that there's no truth to the charge," Henry says. "But he's also telling the levelookers that his daughter isn't even *at* the fair."

"Oh," I whisper, because if one of them sees me, especially with this tray around my neck, it will look like Papa is a liar, even if he simply didn't know better. And if he's a liar about my being here, it'll look like he's lying about sending me out as a strolling peddler as well.

"There's but one thing to do," Henry says. "Give me whatever charms you have left and I'll put them with mine on the counter. When the levelookers call you into the justice tent, you can say that whoever laid the charge was mistaken, that you're just here as a fairgoer and you're not selling anything for anyone."

"I—will not be doing that," I sputter.

"Please." His voice is scared and urgent. "Unless you want your father to be fined. Twice over, if you're caught in the act."

They'd march him into the justice tent, and there I'd be, sniffling and sorrowful, further from helpful than ever.

Once word got out, the other traders might never trust him again. He wouldn't be welcome at the Robin Hood next year or any other. He might not be welcome at the Stourbridge Fair at all. My family will go hungry, and it will be all my fault.

No. Not my fault. Someone carried tales to the leve-lookers, and there's but one soul within ten miles of here who would see this as a situation to turn to his profit, especially at my expense.

But I could swear that Simon never saw me.

"Could you go to the levelookers yourself and explain?" Margaret asks. "You have the armband that gives you leave to sell."

"They'd call Papa in as well, and then it wouldn't matter." Besides, I'm not about to let Simon ruin every-thing. "Well, the only way Papa gets fined is if I'm caught, and I'll make sure I'm not caught."

"You could hide your hair beneath your hood and take off your apron," Margaret suggests. "That embroi-dery at your waist is easy to mark. Or here, I can trade cloaks with you. That might fool them at a glance."

"Or you could sell them," I say.

Henry shakes his head firmly, but Margaret just looks stunned.

"I don't know, Tick," she replies. "They mean so much to you, and I'd hate to foul up your plan."

The idea of handing my tray to someone else feels like a kick to the belly, but it would solve a lot of prob-lems.

"Come now, you're the one with a head for trade." I smile, even though my heart is racing like a hare in the heather. "Just for today. Tomorrow might be different."

Henry faces her, blustering just like Papa. "You've never been to the fair! You have no idea what to do!"

"Neither have you, baby brother," Margaret tells him coolly, "but I've been watching Tick all morning." To me she says, "All right. I'll give it a try, but you don't get to be upset if it doesn't go the way you like."

I nod as I wriggle out of the linen ropes, keeping the breadboard level so the charms don't fall into the dirt. In a trice, Margaret is wearing my armband and holding my tray in front of her with the loops of braided linen over her shoulders and crossed against her back.

She looks a little scared, but a little proud, too.

"At least stand near enough Garlic Row so I can see you," Henry pleads. "It would make me feel better knowing I can step in if you need me to."

"I don't know what you think is going to happen," Margaret replies, but her voice trembles in a way that says she doesn't know, either. "Still, I get to see so little of you these days. Very well. Let's be off."

I hand her my rucksack and she shoulders it easily, but then I don't know what to do with my hands. I twist them in my apron as I watch Margaret and Henry take their leave.

The crowds are dense and growing by the moment, and beyond is the hum of chatter and the smell of roasting meat and the distant plink and chime of music, but I can't look around without wondering who else has recognized me.

In the years we've been coming here, I've been Papa's shadow, following him from stall to stall and standing proudly at his elbow as he talked about roads and tolls and measures with this trader and that merchant.

Every moment I spend here is one that makes it harder for Margaret to sell my wax charms. The best way to keep from being caught is to take myself somewhere the levelookers for sure can't find me.

That's the hostel.

I haven't seen the fortune hen. I haven't eaten spicy meat or watched the tumbling troupe or admired the paternosters made of coral or jade or chalcedony.

But more than any of those things, I want to see the look on Papa's face when I pour silver into his hands. Even if I'm not the one who gathered every coin of it. I want to hear him admire my Agni Dei and praise the cleverness of my Scholastica cats.

With one last long look at the cheerful swirl of color and laughter and music and joy, I turn and head toward Cambridge.

When I get to the hostel, I let myself in the hidden yard gate that Henry showed me, then go in search of

Mistress Bea. If I can't sell wax charms, at least I can make myself useful here, and it will make the time go by faster.

She's not in the kitchen, although the big kettle of stew is already sending up delicious smells, and she's not at the washing trough behind it.

There are voices coming from the hall, then a squeal, then laughter. Boys' laughter. When I step through the doorway, I spot Mistress Bea bending over a young man seated on one of the trestle benches. Two more youths are hovering behind her. One is fair-haired and the other dark. They're wearing fine woolen tunics, and they're in high spirits. The hall is empty but for them, and without guests spilling everywhere, it's cavernous.

"Hold still!" scolds Mistress Bea, which causes the youths to laugh again.

I edge closer. The boy on the bench has a massive cut down his cheek, which Mistress Bea is hovering a needle over. His tunic and hose are a slaughter and his neck is smeared with blood, although it looks like someone tried to wipe it clean. He's older than me, likely older than Margaret, but right now he looks like one of Lucy's or Johanna's little brothers struggling against some mothering.

At first I think they must be scholars, but they're not wearing the robes they strut around in. They must be guests, then, and Mistress Bea must be taking pity on them.

"Twopence he cries before it's done," says the dark-haired youth standing nearby, and the fair one laughs and paws his shoulder like Big Gray giving the Fox a playful blow.

Around the taunter's neck is a Scholastica cat. On a red ribbon. Just like the one I gave to Margaret.

She said she took it off for safekeeping. There's no way other than thievery he might have gotten it. I know the face of every soul who bought a charm from me earlier today, and none of them was a boy with a sunburn and gap between his front teeth.

I storm up and jab a finger at the youth's collarbones. "Where'd you get that?"

He grins and touches the charm lovingly. "What, this? Can't tell you. I'll take the secret to my grave."

"Shove off, Bernard," the other boy says, in the punch-and-elbow way of the boy packs of St Neots.

"Enough, lads," Mistress Bea tells them over her shoulder. "Tick, where's Margaret?"

"She stayed behind. Don't worry, she's, ah, sticking close to Henry."

"Very well." Mistress Bea gestures to a piece of hide curled into a cone at my end of the trestle. "Can you bring me that salve?"

I fetch it over to her. It smells of nettles and long days inside. Mistress Bea dips a finger in the ointment and smears it down the boy's cut. He whimpers but doesn't squeal.

"I know you took that wax charm from Margaret," I tell Bernard, out loud in front of Mistress Bea. "That's thievery."

Bernard presses both hands over his heart as if deeply wounded, but he's still grinning like a halfwit. "What's thievery is the price she wanted for it. A shilling's a lot for a starving scholar, and she never has so much as a whisper of pity for me."

"You're no scholar," I reply, folding my arms. "Scholars are never without their robes."

"Unless it's fair time," his friend replies cheerfully. "It's best if we blend into the crowd. The masters have no liking for us doing anything that might be considered even somewhat fun."

"Apparently, fun is bad for our morality," Bernard puts in, smiling roguishly.

"There." Mistress Bea wipes her hands on her apron. "All patched up. I take it you lads are back into the thick of it?"

"We are going out of doors to settle the question of where Nardo here got the lion of St Mark," says the fair-haired boy.

"You couldn't really have bought that from Margaret," I say slowly, because the idea that she may have valued her Scholastica cat so little is not something I want to consider.

"My hand to God," Bernard replies. "This pizzlewit is just jealous because he's sweet on her."

He shoves the fair-haired boy, whose pale cheeks go pink and then red as his fellows hoot and taunt. He must be Peter, the reason Margaret knows that more than one lamb is *agni*.

"I just want one, too, is all. You're not the only one studying law, you turd." Peter turns to me and asks, "Are you a friend of Margaret's? Do you know where she got the charm? I'll pay a shilling and be a lot more decent about it than this fool."

A shilling. A *shilling*. That's *twelve* pennies for *one* charm.

"Ah." I'm finding it hard to use words. "I . . . could probably get you one. Depending on . . . how things go."

Peter must misunderstand my stumbling, because he rushes on. "St Mark is the patron saint of lawyers, and I could use all the help I can get to find a worthy master and prove myself to him."

"Go, if you're going," Mistress Bea says to them in a motherly but exasperated way, and she shoos the scholars toward the door with her rag.

I glance at Mistress Bea, who may not like knowing that Margaret is at the fair by herself selling wax charms while I dodge the levelookers in her hostel.

So I call after the boys, "Come find me at supper. I might be able to help you."

17

MISTRESS BEA keeps me busy all afternoon scrubbing and fetching, so by the time I look up, the sky outside the kitchen door is a deep purple and Margaret is skipping in grinning like a month of honey cake. Her cheeks are pink from the sun and my rucksack is slung easily over one shoulder, and there's a lightness to her step that sends a quiver of envy through my guts.

She has the look of someone who's been all afternoon at the fair, and I'm the one with blisters from the handle of the leather water bucket.

Still, I make myself smile. "You look happy. It must have been a good day."

"It was the *best*," Margaret replies, hugging the breadboard. "Not just for me, either. For your father and

Henry, too. Can you believe they sold all their candles? Every last one!"

All thoughts of confronting her about selling Bernard her Scholastica cat or warning her about Simon go flying away. "You must be jesting."

Margaret shakes her head cheerfully as she hands over my rucksack and the breadboard. "Your father's delighted, of course. He even gave Henry enough coin to treat me to a meat pie at a cookhouse to celebrate."

In all the years I've been going to the fair, Papa and I have never sold all our candles in one day. Most often we sell the last of them just as the booth is coming down, when people who've put off buying hope they can have a bargain.

"Your father thought I was Henry's sweetheart, can you believe?" Margaret chuckles. "We look so much alike, though, only a blind man would think it. Henry didn't correct him, either. Which means he hasn't said anything about our family yet, the little rotter."

"Oh saints," I murmur. "What if Papa packs up the booth and heads home? I still have so many charms left!"

Margaret shakes her head as she ties on an apron and picks up a stirring paddle. "There are still Henry's Agni Dei. I guess selling the candles in larger lots means your father didn't get as much silver as he would otherwise, and he's hoping to make up the difference with the wax charms. Henry mentioned how you told him that they tend to sell quickly."

They usually do, when they're of a lot higher quality than the ones Henry made.

And when someone else isn't wandering around with better ones.

While Margaret loads a serving bowl with stew, I open my rucksack to take stock of my charms. On top of the linen-wrapped packets is a small kerchief tied with a knot, which opens in my palm as a tumbling of coins.

For the longest moment, all I can do is stare. I've seen coins in plenty before, but none that were solely my own. People thought enough of the wax charms I made to part with silver for them, and soon I will pour these pennies and farthings into my papa's hands, and he will look up at me with wonder writ across his whole face.

There's enough coins to pour, but not as many as I hoped for. Likely Margaret was too shy to properly bellow my wares. At least there'll be plenty of Scholastica cats for the scholars.

"That makes sense, since there's also Henry's learning," I say. "Papa must make sure that Henry can manage himself at the fair, and he'd be wise to use all the time that's given him."

"If one of those lessons is how to face levelookers, I could surely help him study it," Margaret replies. "They came right up to me. Big men, those. Like oxen they were. But I definitely wasn't Osbert Greenwell's daughter and I had a red armband, so they kept moving."

Her hands shake the smallest bit as she cuts rye bread into thick slices and piles them into a basket.

"Did the levelookers say anything else?" I ask nervously.

"They wanted to know where I got the charms," Margaret replies. "I didn't dare say I made them myself. What if they asked how? So I told the levelookers that I bought the charms from a trader who came to the Midsummer fair."

I nod. It's not against the rules to sell something you bought at a different fair.

"I just . . . thought there'd be more," I say, poking a finger through the pennies and farthings in the kerchief.

Margaret narrows her eyes. "You promised to be happy with whatever I brought."

"Oh, I am!" It comes out rushed, like a ewe's blattering. "Only . . . perhaps tomorrow we can try something else. So I don't have to miss any more of the fair."

"Like what?"

"We could trade clothes." For the second time of late, I'm deeply grateful that my every stitch of clothing doesn't smell of tallow.

Margaret laughs aloud. "Tick, your gown would

barely cover my shins. But I think I have an old kirtle you could borrow. I'm just sorry you couldn't stay longer at the fair today. Plenty of people missed you."

I go still. "Ah. People?"

"Well. The boy in the next booth, for sure." She tucks a wooden spreading tool onto the butter plate. "He was most curious to know how you were liking the fair."

I can even hear him say it. That grating, obnoxious simper. The sly, cutting smile. But Simon should have no way of knowing I'm here at all.

Unless Margaret mentioned it earlier, when he stepped into her path. She wouldn't have known not to. She might have told him everything.

I grit my teeth, but I can't be angry. What's done is done, and it's my own fault for keeping secrets from my friends.

Mistress Bea hurries in, telling us that the guests are arriving. She and Margaret and I start ferrying bowls and plates and flagons between the kitchen and the hall. The guests, young and old, are weary after a busy day at the fair, but it's a weariness with a good humor to it, and they're glad at the sight of a meal.

There's no sign of the scholars. Not at table. Not near the hearth. They might be in their undercroft, but I highly doubt they'd miss a supper they've already paid for.

I should have known better than to believe Bernard

when he said he'd paid a shilling for Margaret's charm, and Peter for promising to agreeably pay that price for his own. Blackguards and liars, the lot of them.

"It's not that I think you did a poor job selling," I tell Margaret as we trade empty platters for full ones in the kitchen, even though that is perilously close to what I think. "It's more that I didn't realize how much I wanted to do it myself. It will mean less in the end if I give over coin I didn't earn."

"Besides, the levelookers already had words with me," Margaret replies. "It's highly unlikely that they'll do it again."

"Not when there are so many other scoundrels," I mutter, and I can't help thinking once more of those hungry-looking boys with dark circles beneath their eyes and dozens of candles on their backs.

"Here's an idea," she says. "What if I hold the tray and take the money, and you're the one who does the bargaining? Then you're not exactly the one doing the selling, are you?"

Given how much silver the lepers and their keepers make from fines extracted from people who reason in ways like this, I'm not sure I agree.

But if what Margaret says is true, if Papa didn't get as much money from candles as he usually does and now he's pinning his hopes on Henry's Agni Dei, I must take the risk and put myself in charge of selling my own charms.

Being helpful isn't always easy.

As supper is winding down, Margaret and I place a towering ginger cake onto the biggest platter in the kitchen, and slowly bobble it across the darkening yard toward the hall. My mouth waters with every step. A loud cheer goes up as we ease it through the doorway and onto the sideboard.

Mistress Bea appears with her big knife to cut the cake into wedges. She hands Margaret a flagon of ale, gestures to a hooded guest sitting alone by the fire, and asks her to refill his mug. Margaret hardly takes two steps before she squeals, shoves the flagon at me, and flies toward him.

"Da!" she cries, and his arms close around her so fast and fierce that I have to look away.

One of the guests at the trestle calls for ale, which lets me busy my hands. By the time I refill all the mugs there, Margaret and her papa are deep in the kind of fond conversation that looks so very familiar. He still has his arm around her shoulders, holding her tight against him. Right here in the hall, in front of everyone.

I glance at Mistress Bea, but she's not glaring or stewing. She's merely cutting slabs of ginger cake and settling them on squares of linen for the guests.

Margaret's papa is golden like a lion. He stands like one, too, broad and carefree but without a hint of swagger, like he doesn't feel the need to defend the space he takes up. Whatever she's saying, he's listening like she's the only person in the room.

I help Mistress Bea hand out cake. I keep expecting her to call Margaret over to do her part, but she lets them alone to share news that's been collecting over the months they've been apart.

Once every guest has a piece, I bring some cake to Margaret and her papa. Margaret must have told him who I am, because he grins at me like I grew up in his dooryard.

"Saints, Tick, I can hardly believe it's you!" Margaret's papa says. "I remember a little poppet with stubby braids who ate from the dog's bowl."

I don't remember that, either, but it sounds like something else I'd do.

I tell him I'm pleased to make his acquaintance, then curtsy and excuse myself to help Mistress Bea clear plates and linen. All the while I'm in and out of the hall, Margaret and her papa never stop talking. Betimes I'll hear one of them laugh aloud. It's easy and comfortable, like me and my papa once were, even though Margaret is way more young-womanly than I am.

When the guests are settled, Mistress Bea and I head

to the kitchen to sweep and tidy. Margaret and her papa follow us. There's pandemain bread and rosemary butter and sage cheese and a dish made with mutton and turnips. The grown-ups each have a mug of wine, and Margaret and I have cider.

Margaret's father says I'm to call him Master John. He asks after Papa and Mama Elly and even Trudge, and he thanks me for being so kind to Margaret and showing her around the fair.

"I've got some matters to attend to in town," Master John says, "but I'm looking forward to stopping by Osbert's booth. I wonder if he'll even recognize me!"

I think about my papa's eyesight and manage a weak smile in return.

While the sky outside grows dark, Margaret and her papa talk about old friends from Norwich and how busy the tannery will be after people slaughter their animals at Martinmas and whether Margaret has made any friends in Cambridge yet.

"Tick and I are friends." She darts a glance my way, like she's asking if it's true, and I grin in reply because I'm glad we've grown close. "She doesn't live here, though. More's the pity. But there's . . . well, there's Peter."

Master John claps his hands over his ears in a silly, overdone way. "No! No, there isn't! I'll not hear about any friends named Peter!"

She giggles and pulls his hands down. "Very well. I'll spare your tender ears."

"Another day, sweeting," he replies. "Far, far from now."

I sip my cider. It's hot and tangy with spices. I think about how Margaret said her papa thought she was growing up too fast. How even though she's young-womanly, her father very much wishes she was still a child, but not in a way that's harsh or demanding. An earnest, wistful way, but one that gives her a place to be wherever she happens to be.

Lucy's papa turned into *Father*. So did Johanna's. But Master John is still very much a papa, and it's clear he plans to stay that way, no matter how old Margaret gets.

I'm not sure what turns some papas into fathers, but it seems to happen when they're thinking more about themselves than their daughters.

Maybe it has nothing to do with the daughters at all.

Margaret's old kirtle is yellow, which is not my favorite color, but it's clean and smells of lavender and it's only a little bit too long in both hem and sleeve. She lends me an apron, too, since an embroidered waist is an easy way for the levelookers to mark me. I hand over my red armband, which looks cheerful against her blue sleeve.

"Before we do anything else, I must tell Henry that

Da has arrived," she says as we hurry along the Barnwell road. "I know I should let him take his lumps, but I just can't."

I sigh, but she's right. While she heads off toward Garlic Row, I try to busy myself looking at pretty skeins of wool—only to fall over a boy holding a linen sling that's heavy with candles. His nails are bitten off and caked thick with dirt.

"You want some?" he grunts, holding them up.

The candles are well-made, the tallow rendered nicely to an even shade and the lengths all the same. There must be a new chandler at the fair this year. Someone who does work as fine as Papa's, but who ought to insist his apprentice bathe himself before walking out as a strolling peddler.

"How much?" I ask, because these candles look so much like ours that they ought to command a similar price.

"A penny."

I blink. "*Each?* But that—that's way more than it ought to be!"

"Won't find the like for a better price." The boy shrugs. "Wax candles are a better bargain now."

The boy smells of pigsty, not tallow. There's not a single spatter burn anywhere up and down his bony arms.

"Where did you get these?" I demand.

His whole face goes hard. "Made them."

"You did *not!*" I snap, loud enough to bring several heads around, but the boy is on the move, slipping between shoulders and past elbows and into the crowd, juggling his load.

For the longest moment, I'm frozen in place. Those candles are ours. They have to be. I'd have seen or heard about another chandler by now.

I'm not sure how, but this boy is a thief.

I can't go to the levelookers or the fair wardens, though, and I surely can't go to Papa.

But Henry could.

I turn on my heel and move as fast as I can through the fairgoers. Fortunately, it's less crowded in the fields on either side of Garlic Row, and soon enough I'm creeping up on our tent from behind, where Margaret and Henry are deep in a conversation I'm not sure I should interrupt.

"I know I promised!" Henry is whisper-hissing as I edge near. "I just . . . I can't bear it. It's bad enough when a buyer picks up one of my charms and makes a face like he caught a whiff of privy. But Da doing the same? In front of Master Osbert? I'd be humiliated." His voice goes to a mumble as he adds, "And possibly dismissed."

He glances at my wax charms on the breadboard around her neck and looks away.

Margaret sighs. "Henry . . . you can't keep doing what's easy in the moment to make a problem go away, instead of just facing up to whatever it is. All it does is make the consequences that much worse when you finally do have to reap the whirlwind."

Over Margaret's shoulder, through a gap in the tents, I spot a growing crowd around Simon's booth. No one's supposed to block the thoroughfare, but as is custom, neither Simon nor his father feels the need to follow the rules.

"I can't stop Da from coming here," she warns.

"No, but you could stall him." Henry smiles at her winningly.

Margaret grips the tray hard enough to make the wax charms dance. "If you don't tell Master Osbert, I will."

A woman works her way through the crowd in front of Simon's booth and into the middle of Garlic Row. She's holding a basket with a few wax candles poking out. Her gown is threadbare and her wrists are thin. She doesn't look like the sort of person who'd buy three wax candles instead of a pound of tallow ones.

"What if I invited Master Osbert to supper instead?" Henry asks hopefully.

"Because that would make things go hard for Tick," Margaret reminds him.

"Well, perhaps she should tell *her* father the truth as well!"

The woman with the basket slows as she passes our booth, and her gaze lingers on the bare trestle board where dozens of tallow candles usually lie. She sighs, then keeps walking.

Wax candles are a better bargain now.

"Oh," I whisper, because all at once I see it. That grimy boy was no one's apprentice, but he's no thief, either. Those candles he was selling for ten times what they're worth *were* ours, I'm sure of it, and I think I know how he came by them.

Simon hired boys to buy them all up yesterday in a way where no one was the wiser, and now those vermin are keeping the price high while he and his father sell their wax candles. Once the wax candles are gone, anyone who wants the remaining tallow candles will have to part with whatever coin Simon decides they're worth.

Every last act of that is against the rules.

"I won't let him get away with it," I growl, and I don't realize I've said it aloud till both Margaret and Henry turn toward me. Henry's cheeks are pink, like he wishes I hadn't overheard him insisting I confess, but I'm too upset to care.

Bad enough Simon is breaking the rules for all the wrong reasons. Worse yet is the very real chance that we'll pass this winter eating smaller portions at each meal, shivering a little more to save the wood.

Or perhaps there won't be enough silver left in spring to buy the amount of tallow it will take to make enough candles to recover from this year's loss.

Papa really might send Henry home if he can't feed him.

None of that is going to happen. Not if I can stop it.

I gesture to Margaret and Henry to come close. I tell them everything.

Henry's face goes storm-cloud dark. "I can't believe that Simon made a fool of Master Osbert and me both. The pair of us standing there *thanking* those little rats for their custom. You even *warned* me!"

"I ought to go over there and . . ." I trail off, though, because Simon is likely the one who set the fair wardens on me in the first place. Turning up in a fury to blacken his eye will feel good for a moment, but will only worsen my troubles.

"We'll fetch the levelookers," Margaret says. "If Simon's reselling your papa's candles, he ought to be stopped and punished."

I shake my head. "He'll deny everything. He'll say he bought the candles within the bounds of the law, which is true, and those boys doing the reselling will be the ones punished. Not Simon."

"If the boys were fined, they'd surely tell on Simon," Henry says.

"The fair wardens won't disrupt any trader's business unless there's evidence that they've done something wrong," I reply glumly. "Right now we have none against Simon, nor the boys."

Margaret looks thoughtful. Then she unwinds the breadboard tray from around her shoulders and hands it to me, along with my rucksack. "Very well. I'll get some evidence."

Henry frowns. "Why would he tell you anything?"

She lifts her eyebrows at him, and I remember the moment in the row when Simon put himself in her way and smiled like a wantwit and turned pink like he'd never seen a girl before.

"Absolutely not." Henry grabs for her, but she's already moving through the gap between the tents. He growls a curse, then turns on his heel and dodges through the field, away from Garlic Row.

I think to go after him, but it seems better to give him a moment to collect himself. Besides, I daren't run with a trayful of charms. Instead I move down the row away from Papa's booth, but where I can keep an eye on Margaret.

Sure enough, she's waved Simon out from behind the trestle counter and into the thoroughfare.

I don't know if Margaret and I each had a different growing-up talk, or if just growing up makes you know things like how to get a boy to tell you whatever you want to know, but right now Simon is leaning toward her like a fish on a hook. She's smiling bigger now, like whatever he's saying is the most interesting thing she's ever heard.

"Good," I whisper. "Tell her everything."

At that moment, a cold, heavy hand falls on my shoulder and spins me around. It's a man, big and red-bearded, and there's a levelooker badge pinned at his throat.

"Right, then, sweeting," he says. "Want to tell us why you're selling goods without an armband?"

18

MY MOUTH is open. I'm trying to make words, but none come.

I know this levelooker. He's called Robert, and everything about him puts me in mind of a ham. Papa likes him because he's not above helping someone unload their cart, even fishmongers whose cargo leaves him reeking.

When Robert reaches for my tray, I pull it out of his reach and stumble back, into Peveril. At least once every fair, Peveril and my papa drag themselves back from the Robin Hood late at night, leaning against each other and singing badly like a pair of lovesick tomcats.

"I'm not selling without—" I scrabble a hand to my upper arm where my red armband should be but isn't.

Because I untied it this morning and gave it to Margaret, since she would be holding the tray.

But she isn't now, because she's in the thoroughfare a stone's throw from me smiling up at Simon like she has every intention of letting him steal a kiss.

Robert is peering into my face like he's trying to place me. He and Peveril aren't the only levelookers at the fair, but some of their number were trying to find me yesterday. Perhaps they all sit around the Robin Hood and talk about things like this.

"Bert, aren't these the same wax charms that little bird was selling earlier?" Peveril still has me by the elbow, and now he's peering at the charms lined up neatly on the breadboard. "You remember. The comely one."

"Ahhh, you're right. The lambs are common enough, but I remember those odd cats."

My belly falls down and down, and I leave off struggling. Instead I start to babble. "Right. I know how this looks. I *did* buy an armband, only my friend has it and she's the one you're talking ab—"

"Let me tell you how this looks." Peveril gives my rucksack a shake and it jingles traitorously. "Here you are with no armband and your purse full of silver, while in possession of very distinctive wax charms that another girl was selling yesterday."

"But she was selling them for me!" I protest. "I made these. I can even tell you how!"

Robert shakes his head, slow and disappointed. "Either you're cheating the lepers, or you're a thief. Which is it?"

"Can't we just ask her? She—"

Only Margaret is nowhere to be seen. Neither is Simon. The crowd around Simon's booth has grown larger as people buy wax candles instead of tallow ones that now cost a fortune because Simon decided to whisper in ears, when I *had* an armband and I got it by fair means just like I was supposed to from that monk who—

That monk.

I never went back and redeemed my charm. He still has it, and he'll remember that I was the one who came alone to buy it before the fair even started.

Margaret is missing and Henry is going to be furious.

I can't do anything about that now, and I *can't* be marched into the justice tent and face my papa like this.

"Beg pardon." I glance between the levelookers. "I can prove that I bought that armband and these charms are mine."

Peveril lifts a brow. "Can you, then?"

I nod firmly. "And the rules of the fair say that the accused get a chance to prove their innocence."

Robert almost looks amused. "Very well. Prove away."

○ ○ ○

The monk's not hard to find. He's sitting beneath a tree near the river with his hands folded on his big belly and his bare feet in the sun. There's less call for armbands as the fair goes along, and he's got the remaining strips of red cloth around his neck like vestments.

He looks up as we approach, glances from me to the levelookers at my elbows, and muffles a laugh. "It'll be fourpence now, child. This thing got heavy."

The monk pulls my Agnus Dei from his purse and I all but grab it out of his hands. I swipe another off my tray and hold both out to the levelookers side by side. "See? They're the same. Down to the paintwork."

"Hey now!" The monk shoves a palm at me.

"All right, but tell these men how you got that charm," I reply as I dig coins from the kerchief in my rucksack. "Tell them how I had no silver at the start of the fair and you were kind enough to give me an armband in exchange for an Agnus Dei, that I could come back and redeem."

Robert looks up from comparing the charms. "Is that true, brother monk?"

Once I start counting farthings into the monk's palm, he says, "All true. Charity is a virtue, you know."

Peveril and Robert trade a look, then Robert drops both Agni Dei onto my breadboard. "Well then. That clears up the charge of theft, but even if you bought an armband, you don't have it now."

"Don't you have any pennies?" the monk grumbles, but I ignore him and carefully finish counting sixteen farthings into his palm.

"It all spends the same," I reply, honey-sweet, because both of us know farthings are bothersome to keep track of and what's in his hand is the same as fourpence.

Then I turn to the levelookers. "Let me find my friend. I'll get my armband back from her, and I won't be without it again."

Robert smiles faintly. "I'll go with you."

My smile freezes. If Simon catches sight of a levelooker before he lets something slip to Margaret, he'll know to hold his tongue and we'll never prove his deviltry.

But Margaret might need their help.

"Ahh, Bert, just let her go," Peveril says. "She's a child. There are worse cheats here."

Robert sighs, but shoos me toward the fair. "Mind you get that armband before you sell another thing."

"I will! Thank you, my lord! I—"

I stop, is what I do. Right there in the hustle of the crowd, music and chatter and footfalls all around.

Papa is barreling toward me. Master John is a pace

behind him, and trailing after are Margaret and Henry, who scurry like scolded hounds.

I look down at the tray in my hands. The two rows of charms, Agni Dei on top and Scholastica cats on the bottom.

Where is a storm when you need one?

Henry and Margaret both start talking at once.

"I only fetched the levelookers when I couldn't see Margaret; I had no idea they'd—"

"That scoundrel definitely knows something he's not saying, but there's no way he's going to—"

Papa's bellowing drowns them out. He's never rough with me, but he grabs me by the elbow hard enough to hurt and steers me toward the bottom end of the fair where the justice tent is.

He's as wroth as I've ever seen him. On he goes, on and on about how disobedient I am, how disappointed he is, how much Mama Elly must be worried about me.

This isn't how it's supposed to happen. I was going to fill his hands with silver and show him my work. He was going to hug me and say how he couldn't do without my help.

Now he's reminding me how I made him a liar, that he swore to the fair wardens that I hadn't even come to Stourbridge and *now* what's he going to do?

He was going to admire my paintwork. The cleverness of the Scholastica cats. At the very least he'd have agreed that the extra coins were welcome.

I try to tell Papa about Simon and the reselling of our candles, but he waves it away like a buzzing insect and roars, "None of that matters now! You are going to give an account of yourself. Of *this*."

He stabs a finger at my tray of charms, hard enough that I curl my body to shield them. He looks like he's a blink away from throwing the wax discs into the nearest fire.

I don't reply. I *can't* reply. After the storm, when he learned his sister had died, St Benedict came to realize that God had done him a favor by granting her request. Even though he was upset that he'd been made to break the rules, he saw the good that came of it. He buried St Scholastica in the tomb that had been built for him, so she would be near him always, and so he would remember that goodness for what it taught him.

But my papa isn't like St Benedict. All he can see is how many rules I broke. Not the reasons I broke them.

"Well?" Papa thunders as we near the justice tent. "What have you got to say for yourself?"

It's too late. I should have realized it that first day Henry arrived, when it had already been decided how things were going to be.

"Nothing, Father." My voice trembles. "There's nothing I can say."

He stops. Mouth open. Then he says, "I'm sorry, what was that?"

"I have no way to give an account of myself," I reply in a low, shaky voice. "I did all the things you said. I got beeswax by ill means. I lied to Mama Elly. I used your tools without your leave, I came to the fair on my own, I convinced Henry to hold his tongue—"

"No," he cuts in. "No, you called me *Father*. You never call me that."

A fair warden steps out of the justice tent, frowning in confusion, and my father moves toward him, gesturing to me, to my tray of wax charms, to Margaret who's coming up behind me along with Henry and Master John.

My father and the warden disappear inside the tent.

Henry looks greensick. Master John has a firm hand on his shoulder, like he thinks Henry will bolt like a rabbit. Margaret removes my red armband and hands it to me without a word.

I kneel and slip open my rucksack. One by one, I remove charms from the breadboard, wrap them in their scraps of linen, and stow them carefully.

All that work, for nothing.

Simon will get away with reselling our candles.

And my papa is well beyond my reach. He is my father now. For good.

The fair wardens send him out of the justice tent, then call me in. They want to see if he and I tell the same story.

I might be far gone from needed, but at least I can keep him out of trouble. I tell them the truth: I came to the fair without my father's permission or knowledge to sell charms he had no part in making.

The fair warden gestures to my rucksack, and I pull out a charm for him to look at. It's a Scholastica cat, and he holds it next to an Agnus Dei that's clearly Henry's, complete with shaky painting and uneven varnish.

"Your father didn't make two sets of charms and ask you to sell these on his behalf?" the warden asks.

"No, my lord. I made these with my own hand. My father had nothing to do with any of this." I reach into my apron pouch and pull out the brooch with the Scholastica cat that Lucy's papa made. "See? Here's the mold."

The fair warden blinks. "Saints, my girl! Where does a child get a gold brooch?"

I shake my head. "It's just gilt."

"It most certainly is *not*." The fair warden blows out a long breath and hands it back. "Keep that out of sight, child, or you'll have every cutpurse in Cambridge hulking about."

I close my hand around it. I'd give it back if Lucy

would take it, but she's never going to take it.

The fair wardens agree that there's nothing to the charge that I was selling unlawfully at my father's request, and he was mistaken and not lying when he claimed I wasn't at the fair. They tell me I'm free to go, and neither of us will be fined.

"Will the boy who made this false accusation be punished?" I ask.

"He made a mistake, same as you." The fair warden squints at me. "How did you know it was a boy?"

I didn't for certain, until now. But I force myself to shrug and say, "Lucky guess."

Then I curtsy and step out of the tent, and almost fall over Master John's boots. I'm a little surprised to see him still here, but then I see my father and Henry a little ways distant, deep in conversation.

Henry is studying his feet. My father is ranting like a madman, calling on every saint to heed him.

And I am across the trampled ground and into the middle of it, putting myself firmly at Henry's shoulder.

"You should have *said something*—"

"None of this is Henry's doing," I cut in, even though talking over my father takes my loudest voice. "Please don't dismiss him. I convinced him to stay quiet about all of it. The wax charms. Me coming to the fair. He wanted no part of it."

But Henry says, "No. This *is* my doing. I know my own mind, and I thought to help a friend." He meets my eyes as he says it, but he's trembling all over like he's about to collapse.

It's all I can do not to hug him. Even though hugging boys was very much a part of Mama Elly's growing-up talk, Henry counts as my friend whether he's a boy or not.

My father closes his mouth. He clearly wasn't expecting Henry to say that. He lets out a long, long sigh and presses a hand to his eyes.

"Hey, I've got an idea," Master John says into the silence. His voice is bluff and cheerful. "Osbert, why don't you and Tick come to supper tonight? You've already closed your booth, so let's go see what Bea's got on the fire. I know she's eager to see you. It's been an age!"

Master John hooks a friendly arm over my father's shoulder and leads him away, toward Cambridge. Margaret creeps over to Henry and me, and the three of us trail after at a good distance.

At first we say little, then Margaret clears her throat. "Well, at the very least there are no more secrets."

I nod glumly. Now *everyone* will know I'm a slighted daughter.

"I don't know why Master Osbert didn't simply tell me my charms weren't any good," Henry murmurs. "Does he want to be rid of me? Is that it?"

I almost say, *It's because he can't see well enough to judge.* But that's not my secret to tell.

Then I start to say, *I offered to help but you'd have no part of it.* But that's done and done, and saying as much would just be salt in the wound when there's nothing to do for it.

So I say, "Perhaps you should ask him why. Even if it's not what you want to hear, at least you'll know."

Henry is quiet for a moment. Then he replies, "Perhaps you should do the same."

I study the back of my father where he strides next to his oldest friend. Moving away from me like he's been doing for months now, away from hugs and hair mussing and those endless evenings when we would sip cider and wonder about the world, just the two of us.

I thought I knew why.

Now I'm not so sure.

19

IT'S MIDAFTERNOON with plenty of fair left in the day, so the hostel is empty. The walk seems to put my father in a different mind, because he's all smiles and good cheer when he greets Mistress Bea.

Somewhere along the Barnwell road, Master John must have told him about their situation, because my father asks politely how her venture is going and whether she'd be interested in buying candles when he has a stock once more.

Margaret stabs a glare at Henry. It's easy to know what she's saying. *See? You should have just told Master Osbert. He doesn't care a whit.*

Henry studies his boots.

Mistress Bea puts the three of us to work as usual, and

before long, I almost forget that my father and Master John are lounging in a corner of the hall, drinking ale and sharing the news. The bustle and chaos of supper, the hall full of guests and small children bumping around the room and happy chatter and the clunk of spoons on wooden plates—it's soothing, in a way I'm surprised to reckon.

Partway through the meal, Henry lets out a long breath, hands me a flagon, and says, "Wish me fortune. I'm going to need it."

Before I can ask, he's across the hall, where he puts himself in front of my father.

He'll need more than fortune, so I ask St Scholastica to help him. I'm not the only one who broke the rules for the right reasons.

"Hey! Margaret's friend!" Peter tramples through the door amid a cluster of young men. I recognize Bernard at his elbow, and sure enough, there's Margaret's Scholastica cat around his neck.

I nod coolly to Peter, but he's crossing the room, swaying a little, his face pink and jolly, and he's digging into his purse and holding out a hand to me.

"A shilling, yes?" he asks. "That's the price we agreed on? For a lion of St Mark?"

I'm about to inform Peter that we never agreed on anything of the like when he turns his palm up and there's a heap of pennies.

"May want to count them," Bernard puts in cheerfully. "Boy can't hold his wine."

For the longest moment I just stand there clutching the flagon. Peter hadn't been jesting or lying or mocking. Then I manage, "Ah. Yes. Let me just fetch one for you."

"You have more than one?" Another scholar appears between Peter and Bernard, looking hopeful. He's got an earnest, freckly face and a headful of tight curls. "I'll buy it if you do. Nardo here schooled the master today in the debate and kissed his lion after. A shilling is dear, but I can go without bread awhile."

"Go without wine, you mean."

"Hey, how many lions do you have? I want one!"

I tell the scholars to wait, put down the flagon, and hurry toward the kitchen where I stowed my rucksack. Margaret is slicing bread at the trestle when I rush in, and when I pick up my bag, she looks alarmed.

"You're not leaving, are you?"

"No. Not yet, at least." I hold up the rucksack. "The scholars want to buy Scholastica cats. For a *shilling apiece*."

Margaret flinches. She looks down at her work.

"That Bernard is a crafty one. First he steals your charm, then he convinces his friends he bought it for that ridiculous price. Now they're all willing to pay it." I scowl. "I shouldn't complain, considering it's to my advantage, but I'll not see him leave you with nothing."

I pull out another Scholastica cat and offer it to her.

Margaret is silent, and something cold turns over deep within. "Wait. He *did* steal it from you. You didn't actually sell it to him. Did you?"

"I know what you must think," she murmurs. "That I'm a bad friend. But the truth is that *I'm* the one who didn't think."

My heart flutters.

"Bernard saw the charm around my neck. He asked where I got it, and I explained that it was a gift from a friend. He wanted it. He wanted it *badly* and told me to name a price. So I did. I named the most wild, outlandish price I could think of."

"A shilling," I whisper.

"Fully a week's lodging," Margaret replies. "I thought he'd laugh and leave off. I thought he'd understand that I had no plans to part with it. But when he *agreed*? When he produced the money right there and put it in my palm? What could I do?"

The cat on the charm I'm holding is white. Just like an Agnus Dei lamb.

"I'm sorry, Tick," she whispers. "It was foolish."

I thought the worst of Bernard, even when he told the truth. When he had no reason whatever to lie. It's no different from thinking the worst of Lucy and Johanna.

Or my father.

I come around the trestle to give Margaret a hug, then I push the charm into her hands. Then I shoulder my rucksack, head back to the hall, and trade the last five Scholastica cats for so much silver that it barely fits in my kerchief.

"Come back at Shrovetide," Peter tells me. "When new boys start turning up, tell them you're charging *two* shillings. They'll pay it, and we won't say a thing."

I smile, even though there's no chance I'll ever be back here. After this, my father likely won't let me go to the privy alone.

Henry returns. He's grinning hard enough to break into pieces. "I'm not getting dismissed! I begged Master Osbert's pardon for keeping things from him, and he told me there were going to be so many extra chores I'd barely have time to think my own thoughts, but I can *stay!*"

I never thought I'd be happy to hear Henry say those words, but I am. When something good happens to your friend, you ought to be happy with them, even if you're splintering inside.

"I asked him whether he was keeping me on because of his friendship with Da," Henry continues, quieter. "Considering how I'm not as skilled at chandling as you clearly are."

Hearing him say as much feels good, but it leaves out how skill takes time and effort.

"Master Osbert swore it wasn't true. Then he told me about his eyes. He said if I had the courage to confess and ask his pardon, the least he could do was trust me with that secret." Henry smiles a little. "He also said that anyone willing to risk his future in trade to keep a secret for a friend was someone who would do the same for him."

Just then, Margaret and Mistress Bea bring in the evening's sweet—a huge cake packed with dates and honeyed figs. The scholars let out a raucous, singsong cheer that some of the smaller kids join in on. Henry and I hurry over to help Margaret and Mistress Bea cut it into wedges and bring it around to the guests.

Margaret tries to get me to take a piece to my father, but I can't face him. He's never going to forgive me, not even if I give him every coin.

I don't know why I ever thought silver would be enough to win his approval. I should have learned from Mama Elly that your papa will love you or he won't, but no amount of anything will change his mind.

I should have learned the same from Margaret.

Only I'm going to have to face my father sometime, so it's probably best to do it while he's eating cake that looks this good.

I take two wedges from Margaret, the cloth dipping in my palm. She's already wearing her white Scholastica cat around her neck, and it occurs to me that after all the cats I've sold, all the cats I've given away—to Margaret, to Lucy and Johanna and their sisters—I never thought to save one for myself.

I pull in a deep breath and start across the room.

Master John sees me coming, murmurs something in my father's ear, and by the time I get to the hearth corner, it's just my father and me.

I hand him one piece of cake, then I sink onto the low stool that Master John just vacated, holding the other piece in my lap.

"I know you're wroth with me," I say quietly. "I'm sorry for that."

"I have every right to be." My father's voice is clipped. He doesn't even glance at the cake. "Mostly I'm furious that you've left Eleanor to worry. She's got to be frantic by now."

"She thinks I'm at Johanna's," I reply, but now that the rest of my so-called plan has fallen to tatters, I wonder if someone happened by our house and Mama Elly convinced them to bring her into town in a cart and she went to Johanna's to see the new baby and learned none of my story was true.

My father *harrumphs*, but in a way that says he's

relieved. "That doesn't excuse your behavior, Scholastica."

"I only thought to help." I pull my kerchief of coins from my rucksack and give it a jingle so he knows what it is. "Here. Take it. Everything I made from selling charms. There are more than five shillings in there. Scholars have more money than sense."

My father doesn't reach for the kerchief. He doesn't open his hands for me to pour in the silver. He certainly doesn't open his arms for a hug. He merely looks at me like he just dropped a pearl down the privy.

I pull my kerchief back into my lap. I grip it with both hands.

If this is how things will be, if there'll be no hugs and no hair mussing, I'll simply stop touching him at all. That way I can remember the hugs he once gave me when I was small, while I still counted.

"I didn't ask for your help," my father says. "I thought I made it clear how things were going to go."

I have a single charm left. The Agnus Dei I got back from the monk. I pull it out of my apron pouch and lay it on my father's knee.

"I wish you could see it," I whisper. "It might not change your mind that I don't count. But perhaps at least you could know that my work is beautiful."

My father straightens. "Who says you don't count?"

"Everyone who thinks what a wonderful thing it is

that you have a real apprentice now." I meet his eye steady on. "Father."

He turns the charm over in his hand. "Tick, dear one. I've tried to help you understand. I don't know why it's so hard for you."

"You've had a lot to say on the matter," I reply, "but you haven't done a lot of listening."

"Careful," my father says, his voice an edge, but I've already lost him, so whatever I say now doesn't matter.

I start to tell him, *You took away my tasks and gave them to Henry*, but he's already made it clear why he did that.

Then I almost say, *I just want to do work that matters*, but I remember saying the same to Lucy, and she asked how I could think the work she was putting into her little brothers and sisters didn't matter.

All around me, the hostel hums and bustles with people praising the cake, sharing benches, playing with whipping tops, comparing purchases from the fair. The scholars in the corner are having some sort of contest involving recitations in Latin, and every now and then they cackle and hoot with laughter.

None of this happens on its own. Mistress Bea and Margaret are here to bring the cake and wipe down the benches and sweep the floor clean enough for a top to spin. They feed the scholars and sometimes stitch up their faces when they get into scrapes.

All kinds of work are meaningful.

I think about what I said to Henry, how he should just ask a question honestly and expect an honest answer instead of simply figuring he knows what's in someone else's mind.

That it's better to know the truth, even if it hurts.

"If we have candlemaking, there's always something to bring us together." I can't quite look at my father or force my voice above a whisper. "Without that, there's nothing."

He opens his mouth. Closes it. "Tick, I love you and I will always be your papa, and that alone is enough to bring us together."

"My father, you mean."

He frowns, baffled, and I clarify, "My papa was the one who trusted me to mind the kettle and cut fat. He's the one who cared what I thought. He's the one who said making wax charms would be my task, and he would have praised my work to the heavens even if he couldn't see a stroke of it. My *father* decided what his friends thought of him was more important than any of that."

"Not more important," he says, slow enough that I can tell he's thinking it over as he says it. "Just . . . the way of things."

I don't reply. That was part of Mama Elly's growing-up talk, too, when I told her I didn't want any of these growing-up things to happen. *I'm sorry, lamb,* she said. *It's just the way of things.*

"I'm still upset that you misled everyone." He turns the charm over once again. Runs a thumb over the ridges in the wax. Then he asks, "May I keep it? I want to put it next to your mother's."

I nod, and without hesitating, he pulls out a length of cord, strings it through the loop, and puts it around his neck.

I might have silver to show for most of my wax charms, but I got plenty for the ones I gave away.

This one especially.

"I'd . . . much rather be your papa than your father," he adds quietly.

"I'd rather that, too," I say with such gustiness that he laughs aloud.

Then he opens his arms for a hug, and even though I have to risk my cake by setting it on the stool, I put my arms around his neck and hug him hard, tallow smell and all.

Maybe he can be my papa a little while longer.

When I pull away, I grab my cake off the stool before sitting down again. I take a bite, and it's as good as it looks.

"Right," I say through a mouthful of dates and crumbs, "now we must work out how to get the levelookers to punish Simon for reselling our candles."

Papa shakes his head. "Tomorrow we'll pack up the booth and head home. Henry's charms are not going to sell, and I'll do better to cut my losses."

"But we can't just let Simon get away with it!"

"After being accused myself, I doubt the levelookers will take any claim I make seriously," Papa replies. "Yes, I was cleared of wrongdoing, but how will it look? Especially if you're right and Simon was the one who accused me in the first place."

"Then I'll make the claim," I say, but I was accused as well, and besides, we still have no proof.

"Ill winds are going to blow. Best thing to do is tighten your own cloak." Papa picks up his cake. "Simon will get what's coming to him in the end, but for my part, from now on I'll be using a maker's mark."

I'm not happy about Simon escaping punishment, but I'm so full up with feelings that I can't feel one more right now. Instead I finish my cake and think how much I like it here in the hostel where there's so much cake, even though Margaret told me the cake is to impress the guests and they don't have it every night when it's just the scholars.

It reminds me of the kerchief of silver still in my lap, and when I offer it to Papa again, this time he takes it.

He must expect the kerchief to be lighter, because

he nearly drops it. When he opens it, his eyes get huge. "You weren't jesting. There might truly be five shillings here. Did you turn *felon*?"

But he says it teasing, and I giggle and reply, "Does this mean I'm not in trouble?"

My papa laughs. "Oh Tick. No, dear one. You are still in very big trouble."

20

PAPA DECIDES against leaving right away, preferring to wait until the end of the fair to buy our year's provisions. Traders are inclined to bargain instead of carting things home, which means Margaret, Henry, and I are free to enjoy the last day as fairgoers.

We find the fortune hen, and each of us asks her a question.

Margaret asks whether Peter has a fancy for her. I could have saved her a farthing and told her the answer.

Henry asks whether he'll make a good chandler one day. I could be two farthings richer right now.

When it comes time for me to ask, I hesitate. I already know I'll never be a chandler, that Henry's the apprentice and those tasks are his now. I know why

Johanna and Lucy stopped talking to me, and I helped that get better all on my own.

I want to ask whether growing up will turn out all right, but I know better than to ask a question if it's possible the answer isn't one I want to hear.

So I ask, "Will I come back to the fair next year?"

The hen walks straight to the *Yes* grain and pecks busily.

Margaret and Henry help me choose a brick of fine beeswax to replace what Lucy took. We eat roast goose and try something called silbāḥ, which looks suspiciously like eel but is bright yellow with saffron and so spicy that my eyes water, but in the best possible way.

We watch a tumbling troupe set up and perform. It's the same one as last year, five young men with deep brown skin and bright tunics and hose, and even though they invite a different girl to crouch on the mat while they leap over her, I'm happy for her, because now she'll have stories to tell her friends when she gets home.

Every now and then, we spot one of the grubby boys and their slings of ill-gotten candles, but I take Papa's advice and ignore them. I'm too busy enjoying the fair to let ill winds ruin things.

As evening draws near, the wardens make another proclamation announcing that the fair will end at sunset and that's when all trading must cease. Most of the booths are already coming down, and the last few strolling peddlers are anxiously trying to sell what remains of their goods before dark.

Henry, Margaret, and I make our way up Garlic Row to help Papa with the booth. We're sunburned and tired, and our hands are sticky from too many treats, but all three of us are grinning.

Once we wash up, Papa bids Margaret bundle the bedrolls and blankets while he and Henry unpeg the ropes and roll the horsehide. I'm to fetch Trudge and hitch him to the cart standing behind the booth.

I'm partway to the common pens where Trudge has spent the fair eating grass and breaking wind when one of the grubby boys comes up to me. This one is deeply sun-browned and he's missing two front teeth. He holds out his sling of candles.

"Want some? They're going cheap."

I scowl at him. "No. Go away."

"You can have the lot for two farthings," he says urgently, glancing over his shoulder. "Finely made. Best in Stourbridge."

I almost laugh. He may as well be giving them away.

I make a show of scoffing and try to breeze by him, but he puts himself in my path. "Please, miss. I must get *something* for them."

There are at least six pounds of candles in the sling.

Simon bought these from us at fourpence, and clearly no one bought them at the hideous price he thought to charge yesterday. So he's still got them, and now he thinks to be rid of them before the fair ends. This isn't the only boy with our candles I've seen today, either.

Which means Simon is out shillings, when he thought to make a mountain of silver at our expense.

It's not as satisfying as him being fined and publicly held to account by the levelookers, but perhaps a gooseberries-and-privy lesson will take better.

Trudge seems happy to see me. Or perhaps he's happy to see the apple I brought him. Soon enough he's hitched to the cart and everything is loaded in, and while Papa does a last check of the load, I glance over the Stourbridge common.

It looks so different already, without the crowds and the rows and the peaky roofs of tents, and after three days' worth of footfalls and cart wheels and tent pegs and rubbish, the ground looks rumpled and worn.

But the falling daylight puts a shine of gold over everything, like it's made of joy. The fields sweep gently toward the river and the little ferry that takes you across to Chesterton. Cambridge in the distance is a bristle of spires lit orange.

I'm always sad to leave the fair, but it'll be here next

year, and so will I. The fortune hen said so, and she is never wrong.

It's too late in the day to head home to St Neots, so we stay a night in the hostel as guests of Mistress Bea. She secures our loaded wagon in her storehouse and gives Trudge a generous portion of grain. Master John stays as her guest, too, and the way both Margaret and Henry trail after him makes me a little sad for them, as he'll be gone back to Norwich in the morning.

Perhaps Mama Elly is right and I will change as I grow up, but I will always want my papa close, even if things will never quite be the same between us.

There are only a few guests tonight, and the scholars have come and gone by the time we sit at table. There's good stew and plenty of fresh bread and the kind of cheerful, pleasant conversation that makes me wish Mama Elly were here, so it would really feel like a family supper.

When Master John upends his mug, I'm out of my seat and at the sideboard for the flagon before he even asks. Mistress Bea chuckles as I pour him a golden sluice of new ale.

"I'm surely going to miss your daughter, Osbert," she says. "I've never met anyone better suited to working in a hostel. The last few days would have been impossible without her help."

Mistress Bea might be talking to Papa, but she glances my way and smiles.

"Perhaps Tick could stay in the hostel next year at fair time and help with the guests," Margaret says.

I set down the flagon and retake my seat on the bench next to Papa. I don't dare look at him with anything like hope. He's not as angry as he was—not after my shillings bought provisions in plenty with enough left over for some luxuries—but now is not the time to ask anything of him.

"Let's not forget that you still owe me an apprentice," Master John teases. "There are worse trades than keeping a hostel."

"Few better for a woman who knows the value of her own work," Mistress Bea says, and this time she is looking right at me.

A strange little quiet falls over the table. I'm not sure I heard what I thought I heard, but I think Mistress Bea just invited me to come work at the hostel with an eye toward learning how to run one. Not only at fair time, either, but all the time.

Like an apprentice might.

Papa doesn't reply. He lifts his mug and takes a drink.

I'm all but quivering because if I stayed here, I'd never be far from the bustle and busyness of Cambridge. I could go to *three* fairs every year and Margaret could show me everything that's worth seeing and maybe Peter would teach me some Latin, too, even if he's not sweet on me.

"I'd be willing," Papa says slowly, "but there are two others who must agree. One is Eleanor. The other is Tick herself." He turns to me. "Tick, what say you? Would you like to learn this trade from Mistress Bea? Or would you like to think about it?"

If I stayed here, I could learn a trade of my own. One where being young-womanly would matter little. One there would always be a need for.

There's Mama Elly, though. She's not happy if she's not fussing over something, and she will miss me like her right arm.

But she's the one who gave me those growing-up talks, and it was so I'd be ready when these moments came. So when it was time to make a good choice, one that was right for me, I wouldn't grasp at foolishness.

"I have no need to think about it," I say. "I want to come here. I want to be Mistress Bea's apprentice. Can I start right now?"

Papa puts down his mug and musses my hair. "No, dear one. You have accounts to settle at home first."

The hardest thing I have to do is tell Mama Elly everything. At first she cries because she's hurt. Then she listens. Then she hugs me and cries because she's happy and gives her blessing for me to go.

"I told you you'd change your mind about growing up," she says as we sit at the table with mugs of mint tisane.

"I have not," I tell her firmly, but perhaps I have. A child can't take an apprenticeship and leave home to live with someone else's family, even a family that all but feels like your own.

"I'm going to miss you," I whisper, because I'm remembering how Henry cried quietly those first few nights in the loft, and I'm not sure how easy it will be for me once I'm in the hostel.

"Of course you will, and I'll miss you," Mama Elly says in a breezy way, "but it's a mere day's walk to Cambridge, for goodness' sakes. You're not going to Cathay. We'll see you for holidays, and other times for sure. After all, Henry's here. His mama misses him just as much as yours will miss you."

She hugs me again and sends me to Lucy's for the second thing I have to do—turn over the brick of beeswax I bought to replace the one she stole, confess to the goldsmith, and beg his pardon.

It goes as well as you'd think it might.

The last thing I have to do is return the breadboard to Johanna. I find her and Lucy at the millpond. Their little brothers and sisters are playing tug-o-war with a ratty length of rope since the water is too cold to play in.

When I hand the board over, Johanna holds it against her chest like a hug. She's wearing her Scholastica cat around her neck. So is Lucy. I run my thumbs across my embroidered waistband and smile.

"Your father knows about the beeswax," I tell Lucy. "I gave him finer wax than you took and told him you had no hand in it, but I'm not sure he believed me."

She scowls, narrows her eyes. Her papa is long, long gone.

I pull the gold brooch out of my apron pouch. "You should have this. He's rather angry about the whole affair. Giving it back might make things go easier for you."

"And deny others the blessing of Scholastica?" Lucy grins, but it's the smile of someone who knows the whirlwind is coming. "Nah. You keep it. Make as many charms as you can. There are too many slighted daughters in the world. He doesn't get to stop us."

I close my hand around the brooch. Cats are definitely the perfect patron for slighted daughters. They know exactly who their friends are. They have no time for just anyone.

They are more loyal than they seem.

Growing up means one thing for me and something

else entirely for Lucy and Johanna. It might be the way of things, but I don't have to like it.

"Mama's in labor now," Johanna says. "I know it's your punishment and everything, to come over every day and help, but it'll be nice to see you."

Six whole months of diaper washing and endless walking to soothe a wailing baby. Papa thought to make me clean our byre and those of our five nearest neighbors, but Mama Elly knew exactly what would help me remember what the wages of disobedience and falsehoods would be.

But at the end of it will be spring, and in spring I'll be going to Cambridge. There's still a part of me that wishes I'll be in the yard with Papa, waiting for those first bags of fat to trim. Waiting to see those three familiar furry scoundrels turn up one by one. The sun on my shoulders. Everything fresh and greening.

It'll be hard to leave St Neots, but Henry will be here for Mama Elly to fuss over, and he'll get better at chandling every day until he's a master of the trade, same as Papa. Lucy and Johanna have each other and always will, but they'll hug me hard and chatter harder when I come to visit at holiday time. Trudge needs very little to be happy, and Big Gray and Sunshine and the Fox don't need me to tell them exactly when to come around the yard.

But the sun shines on Cambridge, too, and Mistress

Bea's garden is sure to need someone with a hand for growing things. In a town full of scholars, there's always bound to be something happening. I can hardly wait.

But the sun shines on Cambridge, too. Mistress Bea's garden is sure to need someone with a hand for growing things, and the hostel could definitely do with a kitten. In a town full of scholars, there's always bound to be something happening.

I can hardly wait.

J. ANDERSON COATS is the author of *The Many Reflections of Miss Jane Deming, R Is for Rebel, The Green Children of Woolpit, The Night Ride*, and several books for teen readers. Her books have won two Washington State Book Awards, been selected by the Junior Library Guild, and earned rave reviews. Visit her at jandersoncoats.com.